FREEDOM

THE 707 SERIES

4 of 4

RILEY EDWARDS

D1519787

FREEDOM
A Black Ops Romance
Book 4
The 707 Series

Cover design: Riley Edwards

Written by: Riley Edwards

Published by: Riley Edwards

Edited by: Cindy Wolken

Freedom – A Black Ops Romance

First edition – March 3, 2018

❁ Created with Vellum

This book is dedicated to all the brave men and women who serve or have served in the United States Armed Forces. There are no words to properly convey the sacrifices they make and the appreciation I have for the cost of their service.

To my husband. I wouldn't want anyone else by my side on this crazy train called life.

To my children.

A special thanks to the sailors aboard the USS Nimitz (CVN68). I wrote this series while thinking about her crew, especially my daughter who was deployed aboard in support of Operation Inherent Resolve when I started book one. Welcome home sailors! A job well done! BRAVO ZULU!

To the men in the 3rd ID Rock of Marne – **Raider Brigade** - Fort Stewart, Georgia: The 1st Armored Brigade Combat Team, 3rd Infantry Division have completed their training in preparation for their

deployment in support of Operation Resolute Support
may God be with you as you deploy to Korea. –
Dogface soldiers, CAN DO!

Shades45: Be safe, be brave, and stay strong. We love
you and are so proud to call you son. No good-byes
only, "See ya laters."

The world lost 31 Heroes 06 Aug 2011. SOC SEAL
John W. Faas was among the crew that died that day.
Even in death, John continues to inspire all those who
knew him and love him. He is not forgotten - never
forgotten. His sacrifice and that of his family's
reminds us that freedom is never free.

We sleep soundly in our beds because rough men
stand ready in the night to visit violence on those who
would do us harm.

Whether it was the writer George Orwell, the essayist
Richard Grenier, or the Washington Times columnist
Rudyard Kipling who originally wrote those words
matters not. The sentiment rings true. We are only
afforded the luxuries we have because rough men are
willing to stand at the ready. Chief Faas was one of
those men.

31 heroes – From a grateful nation.

1

Holy sweet mother of God!

That was my first thought.

My second was holy fucking hell, that ass!

Sam Hunt's "Body Like a Back Road" was blasting on the stereo and all my intentions of busting Jasper's balls for playing chick music fled and were replaced with the aforementioned notions.

The sexy woman in front of me - who was currently in some bendy yoga-inspired pose - most certainly had the body that had inspired Sam Hunt to write the song.

Sweet Jesus. Those legs.

I wasn't one for going slow as the song suggested, but curves like those? They were made to explore – slowly, diligently, and thoroughly. Toned, tanned legs like that were made to wrap around a man's waist and hold tight. An ass that was more than a handful - tight yet would still ripple as you took her from behind. Or maybe it wouldn't, and my overactive imagination and underused cock were just hoping that's what it'd do. God knows it would be a tragedy if it didn't.

The song changed, and the new singer crooned on about how he'll never settle down and how he doesn't dance. The woman in front of me straightened; her blonde hair pulled up in a knot on the top of her head, not giving me any indication how long it was but exposing a sexy tattoo on the back of her neck. Suddenly I felt like a dick for eye fucking the girl.

I cleared my throat, hoping to get her attention, but between the music and the amount of concentration it must've taken to balance on one leg the way she was, she hadn't heard me.

With both feet now planted firmly on the ground, she looked like she was getting ready to bend over again. I had to stop her. I was in a pair of athletic shorts that would, in no way, conceal a hard-on. And if she bent over in front of me again, I'd be able to pound nails with my cock.

I thought about just slipping out of the room and

going across the lawn and knocking on Jasper's door. She'd never know I was here and I wouldn't have to bother her.

That's what I had planned to do until Jasper yelled my name from his deck and the woman turned and fell forward when she saw me.

"Whoa. Careful," I said and reached out my hand to steady her, catching her hips as she stumbled.

She turned, and I realized the first two thoughts I'd had about this woman did not do her justice. She was even more stunning from the front. Brownish-green eyes stared at me, wide and in shock. Her full lips were parted ever so slightly like she had been getting ready to say something. Beads of sweat dotted her impressive cleavage and disappeared down under her sports bra.

"I, um, didn't know... Sorry. You scared me," she stammered and pulled her hand out of mine.

Had I really been holding on to the poor girl's hand? What the hell was wrong with me? And why the fuck did I have the urge to grab her hand again? The brief contact wasn't enough; I wanted more.

"No need to apologize. I'm the one that's sorry. I was looking for Jasper. I didn't mean to interrupt," I told her. "I'm Clark, by the way. I work with Jasper."

"Right. He's mentioned you. I'm Reagan. Nice to meet you."

Reagan.

Liz's little sister Reagan.

Well, fuck me. Totally and completely off limits.

"You, too. I'll let you get back to your work out."

It was difficult, but I didn't allow my eyes to move from her face. As desperate as I was for one more look, I didn't do it. Instead, I turned on my heels and hightailed it out of the too-small space like a pussy and nearly ran into Jasper.

"You ready?" I asked.

"Yeah. Let me see if Reagan is."

"Reagan?"

What the hell? Jasper and I were going to the boxing gym, did she need a ride somewhere?

"She's coming with us to work out."

"She is?"

"What the fuck is wrong with you? Did you forget how to speak, or are you having issues understanding the English language?"

I didn't know what my problem was. I'd never acted like a stuttering teenager around women, not even when I was a teenager.

"Do you think that's a good idea? The boxing gym this time of day is gonna be filled with nothing

4

but meatheads. They're gonna trip over their dicks when she walks in looking like that."

Jasper threw his head back and roared with laughter. "Like you are?"

Fucker.

"Seriously. What the fuck are you thinking?"

"Good thing we'll both be there then. She'll have two big brother types to watch her back."

Big brother? Did he just say big brother? Because the last thing I was feeling toward Reagan was anything close to brotherly.

Reagan was quiet on the short drive to the gym. She sat in the back of my Jeep, content in her thoughts, while Jasper and I talked about the new training rotation we were starting today. I liked that she didn't need to be the center of attention but interjected when she had something thoughtful to say.

Where the hell had that come from? What did it matter what I liked? I shouldn't like anything about her.

The next two hours were torture. I was in hell. Every buffed-out gym-rat in the room couldn't keep their eyes off Reagan. Not that I could either, and more than that, I shouldn't have cared - but I did.

"Hey, Rea. Come jump in the ring with Clark

while I get a drink," Jasper called ringside to where Reagan was standing, watching us now that she was done with her bag work.

I didn't know if Jasper was punishing me, or if this was his way of keeping Reagan away from the other men in the room. Her small frame slipped through the ropes easily, and all the impure thoughts I had earlier came rushing back with a vengeance. Not that they had been far from the forefront of my mind. Only now, my cock was being strangled by the cup I was wearing. What could I say? My dick had good taste, and Reagan looked positively edible.

"Sorry to intrude on your workout," Reagan said, coming to a stop in front of me.

She couldn't have been more than five feet three. I had almost a full foot on her in height and at least doubled her weight. She was a little thing; the words fun-sized popped into mind along with all the fun things I could do with her.

"You're not intruding. I hope you're not uncomfortable around all these idiots."

"They don't bother me. I'm kinda used to it. Back home, at my old gym, the guys either hit on me the entire time I was trying to work out, or they were offended I would dare enter a boxing gym and made it known women weren't wanted invading their space."

I didn't know why that pissed me off, but it did.

"What got you into boxing?" I asked.

I'd never met a woman that was interested in any sport where there was a good amount of blood involved.

"I don't want to tell you; you'll laugh," she said, tucking her head.

I wanted to touch her, lift her chin and make her look at me.

"Now you have to tell me. I won't laugh. Promise."

She raised her eyes to mine and twisted her lips. How fucking adorable was this girl? Adorable? What the hell was she doing to me? I didn't use words like adorable. I don't even think kittens or babies are adorable.

"When I was in high school, there was this boy, and I wanted to impress him, so I started boxing." She stopped and was trying her hardest to bite back a smile. She lost the battle and her face split into the most devastating smile I'd ever seen. "Sorry. I'm fucking with you. I couldn't keep a straight face, so I ruined it." She covered her mouth to hide her smile, and I wanted to demand she lower her hand and never hide from me again.

I chuckled when she continued to laugh behind her gloved hand.

"So, you know how to spar?" I asked.

She nodded her head.

"Do you want to go a round? Promise to pull my punches."

She stopped laughing and stood straight, steel infusing her spine as she stared me down.

"You better not. It'll piss me off if you do."

"Damn woman, I didn't mean to offend you, but you do realize I outweigh you by at least a hundred pounds, right? I'm not being sexist here; I'm being real."

"If you have to take it easy on me then I have no business being in the ring with you," she replied.

Someone had messed with her head if that's what she thought. Size mattered, especially in sparring. I was six feet two inches and two hundred pounds. I could hurt her in a matter of seconds if I wanted to, and not because of my training, simply because I was so much bigger than her.

"You know there are weight classes for a reason, right?" I asked.

"Do you think some man who finds me in a back

alley is going to pull his punches or care that he outweighs me? Besides, weight classes are for sissies."

I didn't know her well enough to know if she was joking or not. On the one hand, I was impressed with her fire, on the other, I wanted to straighten out her line of thinking. But again, I didn't know her well, and it wasn't my place. And she was right, if someone was trying to harm her they wouldn't go easy on her.

"Then call me a sissy and let's go a light round for points. Hands only?" I asked.

We both had sparring gloves on, but neither of us had on shin guards. Shin-on-shin contact hurt like a bitch, and it didn't matter how careful you were, it was inevitable.

"You're on," she answered, and took an open fighting stance.

One leg back, knees slightly bent, and an even, low center of gravity. Interesting, she'd had some martial arts training as well.

We'd danced around each other for a few minutes before I saw an opening. A quick one-two combination, I tapped her solar plex and waited for her to drop her hands in an effort to block my punch. When she did, I landed a jab to her cheek.

"Damn, you're quick," she said, shaking off my strike.

"That's a first," I laughed.

"What is?"

"Hearing a woman tell me I'm quick."

"Charming."

Her hands came back up, and she threw a wide, arching right hook. I easily ducked her attempt but was too late to block the snap of her round kick to my face. My neck snapped left, and I tasted blood.

Goddamn that was hot. What the hell was wrong with me?

"Shit, sorry. I didn't mean to do that. You said hands only."

I straightened to my full height and looked down at Reagan. Her hair was a matted, sweaty mess, her face was red and blotchy from exertion, and with all that, she had to have been the sexiest woman I'd ever laid eyes on. I couldn't stop myself from wondering if this was what she looked like after sex.

"Now you owe me dinner," I told her.

"What?" She laughed. "Why would I owe you dinner?"

"The first to draw blood has to buy the other person dinner."

"Is that a rule?" She'd stopped dancing around and was fidgeting with her glove.

"It is now."

I knew I had no business flirting with Reagan. I certainly had no business going out to dinner with her. Yet, I absolutely was going to do it. Maybe after I spent some time with her, she'd do something or say something that would show her true colors. All women did. With some it took an hour, with others, it took days, or in my ex-wife's case, it took years. But sooner or later the pretense fades.

That's what I needed.

Once she showed me who she really was, I'd be able to stop this weird fascination I seemed to have.

It was only a matter of time.

2

What was happening right now?

Was Clark flirting with me? Asking me on a date? Surely he wasn't. The man was, H.O.T, hot. (Yes, with all capitals!) No way would he ever look twice in my direction. He was just being nice to me because I was Jasper's friend.

"How do you feel about pizza and beer?" he asked.

"In general, or are we talking specific styles and brands?"

What was wrong with me? Why did I always have to be so lame when I was nervous? And why was I nervous in the first place? That's right, because Clark was hands down the most beautiful man I'd ever laid eyes on.

"In general." He chuckled.

"In general, I love pizza, and as long as the beer is cold and American, I'm game."

Clark wiped the blood from the corner of his lip, drawing my eyes down to his shorts where he'd cleaned his thumb on the fabric. His thighs were big and thick, the size of tree trunks. And I couldn't help concentrating on the area between those huge redwoods and wondered if the rest of him was just as large.

He cleared his throat, and I froze. The problem with that was my eyes had also become immobile, and they were glued to his crotch. He'd caught me. There were no two ways about it. And me being me, I did what I always did, and blurted out the first thing that came to mind. It was normally inappropriate and embarrassing.

Case in point, I opened my mouth and said, "Your thighs are the size of my waist. I don't think I've ever seen legs that big in real life. How many days a week do you work your legs?"

Clark's chuckle turned into an out-and-out laugh, and I was properly mortified. I looked around the room for no other reason than to not look at him, pretending I hadn't just inserted my foot so far into my mouth I wished I would gag on it and end my suffering.

"Hey! You two ready to bounce? Emily just called, and she's upset. I have to get home," Jasper said from the side of the ring.

"Is she hurt?" Clark asked, moving to the ropes. He held them open for me to climb through, but he never took his eyes off Jasper.

"No. Wedding stuff. She was crying, and I could barely understand her. Something about a fire and the venue and needing to postpone the wedding."

Damn. That sucked. I knew how much both Emily and Jasper were looking forward to getting married. Last night Emily had shown me all the plans for the wedding. The bed and breakfast they'd picked was perfect. They'd rented out the entire manor house so Lenox and Lily, Levi and Blake, Clark, and myself could all have rooms at the hotel. We could stay and party all night and not worry about driving. There was also a room reserved for the nanny, so the kids would be on premises, but their parents could still have fun. The next morning Emily had a huge breakfast planned. Poor Emily; she had to be crushed.

None of us bothered to shower before piling into Clark's Jeep.

"Call the hotel and see if we all pitch in and help can they get up and running in time for the wedding," Clark suggested.

"Thanks man, but Em said they might not be reopening."

I remained quiet in the backseat, wishing there was something I could do for Emily and Jasper. I was touched that Clark would come up with something as thoughtful as helping the hotel rebuild so Emily could still have the wedding on time. After everything that Jasper had been through, he deserved this. As crazy as it sounded, my sister Liz would be happy for Jasper, and she'd adore Emily and Jason. They were perfect for him.

Damn, I missed my sister. All these years later, there was still an ache in my chest. Liz was my best friend, my confidant, my protector and losing her the way we did was excruciating. There were no heartfelt goodbyes or last words. One minute she was delivering my stillborn niece, which was heartbreaking enough, and the next she'd coded and was gone. That fast. In one afternoon, both my niece and sister were dead. Jasper's daughter never even drew her first breath or opened her eyes. She was born sleeping; an angel too perfect for this world.

"Reagan?" Jasper's voice broke my musing.

"Yeah?"

"Is that okay?"

Was what okay? What the hell had I missed?

"Sorry, I spaced out. What was the question?" I asked.

"Clark suggested inviting everyone over for pizza to try and cheer Emily up. Do you mind?" Jasper repeated.

"Of course, it's your house."

"I don't want to overwhelm you on your first night here. The guys can be... a lot to handle," Jasper explained.

It was nice of him to be concerned. It was even nicer that he and Emily had opened their home to me and were letting me crash there before I went down to Florida to start my new job. My apartment wouldn't be ready for two more weeks, and I didn't start work for a week after that. As much as I loved my parents, I didn't want to move in with them, even if it was only for a couple of weeks. Since we'd lost Liz, my mother had turned into somewhat of a hoverer, and she'd always been a little overbearing. Who was I kidding? A little? My mother was downright bossy. She meant well, but after a few days, it was too much.

"I'll be fine, Jasper. Besides, I'm looking forward

to meeting everyone. Emily talks about them all the time. Levi and Blake just got married, right?"

Emily had told me all about Lenox and Lily, and Levi and Blake. What she'd failed to mention in any of our conversations was that Clark was drop-dead gorgeous.

"They did. A few weeks ago. The day she moved down here from DC. Levi is a tad bit impulsive when it comes to Blake," Jasper told me.

"A tad? That's an understatement. Levi is completely unreasonable when that woman is around," Clark added.

"That's sweet." I wish I had someone that loved me so much they became irrational around me. I'd never had that. All the guys I'd ever dated turned out to be complete assholes. I had a knack for it. If there was a douchebag in a fifty-mile radius, I'd find him, then he'd latch on to me, and I'd let him bleed me dry emotionally. But that was the old Reagan. The new Reagan was never going to be a doormat again. I was holding out for the perfect man, and until I found him, I was keeping my heart locked deep. But that didn't mean I wouldn't mind having a little fun in the meantime.

"She'll fit right in with the women," Clark said.

When I looked up, I caught Clark staring at me

through the rearview mirror. What was it about this man that sent shivers through my body? Why did it feel like he could see more than I wanted him to? I quickly glanced away, embarrassed that I'd locked eyes with him.

I didn't bother replying to Clark's comment. I was nervous enough meeting everyone; I didn't want to know why he thought I'd fit in. His statement should've made me feel better, but for some reason, it didn't. What if they didn't like me, or they all thought it was weird that I was there? Emily had said that the group was tight; they were family. I was the sister of the mother of Jasper's daughter. He and my sister had been high school sweethearts who'd continued to be close friends after they'd broken up. And obviously, they'd continued to have sex as well. I knew he never loved Liz the way he loves Emily, but he had loved Liz in a best friend sort of way. Maybe this was a really bad idea, me being here. Everyone was going to think it was strange. Sure they'd smile and be nice, but deep down they'd think I was an intruder. Liz's friends always did. She was three years older than me. When we were young it wasn't so bad, but when she was sixteen, and I was thirteen, her friends made it known they didn't like her little sister tagging along. Liz had always told me *she* didn't mind, and not to pay attention to them. After a while I stopped hanging out with her; I felt too much like an annoying hanger-on. I'd overheard a few of her friends saying they were happy I'd finally found my own friends. I hadn't. I found books and would lock myself in my room and get lost in the pages. It was hard living in my popular, outgoing sister's shadow. Not that she did it on purpose, but Liz was...vibrant. Everyone loved her. I was just... me. Awkward and shy.

Shit. Was that what I was doing now? Tagging along with my sister's ex and his friends, even though she wasn't here anymore.

Clark pulled into Jasper's driveway and, me being Reagan, I blurted out exactly what I was thinking. "Maybe I should head down to Florida and stay with my mom and dad."

Jasper turned in his seat and asked, "Why would you do that? If it's too much having everyone over, we don't have to."

Gah! Of course, Jasper would think that was the reason.

"I don't want to intrude."

"Reagan, you're not intruding. Emily and I want you here. She is so excited; it's all she's talked about for weeks."

Damn, damn, damn. I couldn't bail now and have Emily think I was leaving because I was uncomfortable (though I kind of was now that I was thinking about the situation) and I didn't like her.

"If you're sure."

"I'm positive," Jasper smiled at me before he turned in his seat and opened his door.

I wondered if Alesha would've had his smile or my sister's? Jasper was a good-looking man. In high school, all the girls were jealous of Liz since Jasper was the "it" guy in our town. Every girl tried to catch his attention. But one thing about Jasper Walker, he was a one-woman man. He'd never glanced at another girl.

Jasper's door slammed shut, the loud sound making me jump in my seat.

"Why don't you shower and change. I'll pick you up in thirty minutes," Clark said.

"Pick me up? Why?"

"Pizza and beer."

"Umm. I thought everyone was coming over here."

Was he serious about me having to buy everyone dinner?

"Well, seeing as we've established you're good with pizza in general, but we never discussed specific styles and brands of beer, I'm thinking you better come with me."

Something had changed in Clark's tone. He wasn't playful and flirty anymore; he'd turned almost cold but in a friendly way. A friendly cold tone? Did that even make sense? Why was I thinking about Clark's tone anyway and why was I disappointed?

"Sure. Sounds good." I tried to sound upbeat. I obviously failed; Clark frowned and gave me a nod but said nothing else.

———

THIRTY MINUTES later Clark was in Jasper and Emily's living room, and I was pulling on my cutest pair of knee-high leather boots. I adjusted my socks, making sure the top inch peeked out from where the boots stopped, then smoothed down my dress and checked myself in the mirror. Shit, maybe I was over-dressed. My outfit was cute but casual. A cotton long sleeve flowy dress that came down almost to the top of my boots. I'd put on a few chunky long necklaces to dress up the outfit a little without it looking over the top. Would they think I was trying too hard? Maybe I should change into a pair of jeans and my chucks.

Why was I always so indecisive?

"Rea. Clark's here," Emily called from outside the bedroom door.

Too late now.

"Coming." I grabbed my purse and opened the door, almost running smack-dab into Emily. "Damn. Sorry."

"Wow. You look so cute. I totally wish I could pull off an outfit like that," she said, then added, "Clark won't be able to keep his eyes off you."

Was she crazy? Emily was stunning - she had a body to die for. Not to mention, the girl had black hair and blue eyes (*hello*) and a perfect complexion that made me feel like an ugly duckling standing next to her.

"Girl, you're nuts. I'd trade you my dress for your blue eyes in a New York minute. You can borrow the dress if you want."

Emily didn't respond but instead stared at me, and I struggled not to squirm. What was it with her and Clark? Why did they both look at me like I was a zoo animal?

"I'm really happy you're here," Emily said and grabbed my hand. "Really happy. Jasper is too. You're family Reagan, don't forget that."

I was going to kill Jasper. He'd shared. The last

thing Emily needed right now was to worry about my feelings. She had a wedding crisis to deal with.

"Thank you. I'm happy to be here."

What else could I say? Emily and I were still getting to know each other and we'd yet to address the elephant in the room – Liz and Alesha.

"Come on, Clark's waiting." Emily wiggled her eyebrows.

Oh no. I knew what that meant. She was playing little matchmaker.

"You know that Clark is just being nice, right?" I whispered.

"Clark isn't *nice*, Reagan."

What the hell did that mean? He'd seemed perfectly pleasant earlier. I was the queen of the asshole-magnets, but there was no way Jasper would be best friends with a dick, and he'd never allow one around Emily and Jason.

"What are you trying to say?" I asked.

"You'll learn these men are a lot of things; however, *just nice* is not one of them. Protective, bossy, take charge – yes."

"Now you're kinda scaring me. And Jasper is nice."

"Jasper is not nice. He is thoughtful and gentle with those he loves."

"Isn't that the definition of nice?" I asked.

"No. It is something else entirely. There is no defining these men. It's not something I can explain to you. You'll have to learn it on your own."

"Yeah... definitely terrified now."

"Don't be. Hold on tight and enjoy the ride."

Emily had lost her ever-loving mind. I had no idea what the hell she was talking about.

"There is nothing going on with Clark. I promise."

"Okay." She laughed.

When we got into the living room, Clark and Jasper were both standing looking at something rolled out on the kitchen table. The moment they noticed us, Jasper quickly rolled up the papers. Maybe they'd been looking at secret wedding plans and didn't want Emily to see.

I smiled at the guys thinking Emily was wrong – they were nice.

"Ready?" Clark asked.

I tried to ignore the annoyance that was rolling off him in waves and looked back at Emily who was weirdly smiling.

"Sure am. Let's hit the road, Jack." I turned to Jasper. "See ya in a while."

"Yeah."

Great, now Jasper sounded weird too. This was such a bad idea – all of it.

Clark made it to the passenger door before I did and opened it.

See? Nice.

"Thanks," I muttered and got in.

When he started the Jeep, Ozzy Osbourne's "Crazy Train" was blaring through the speakers. I couldn't stop the laugh that escaped.

"Sorry," Clark said, turning the volume down. "You can change the playlist if you want."

"No, it's fine. I love Ozzy."

"Seriously? Aren't you a little young to like him?" Clark asked.

"As if! I snuck out to L.A. when I was sixteen to catch the Black Sabbath reunion tour. My parents were so pissed; I was grounded the entire summer. But it was so worth it."

"Christ."

I didn't know what that meant, so I remained quiet and listened to the song, thinking how I was definitely on a crazy train and it was moving at full speed, and fast approaching the station.

We pulled into a mom and pop pizzeria, and Clark declared, "Best pizza in Georgia."

"Is there such a thing?" I asked.

"What's that?"

"Best pizza. I mean, we're in Georgia. Best pizza is normally reserved for describing pizza in New York or Jersey, or even Chicago. Now they have great pizza. Montana, not so much. We have a chain store pizza which is only a step up from the frozen kind. I would imagine Georgia is the same way."

Clark's lips twitched like he thought my little outburst was amusing instead of what it was – embarrassing. Why did he make me so nervous that I had verbal vomit spew every time I opened my mouth around him?

"When you said you like pizza in general, I hadn't realized you were a connoisseur." Fuck. I was so dumb. "Hey. Look at me," he demanded. "I'm just joking with you."

"Okay."

Something flashed across his face before his smile returned.

"Come on, and prepare to be wowed."

I got out of the Jeep and prayed I'd be able to refrain from saying anything else that would make me sound like more of an idiot.

And why did I care so much what he thought of me? I was here for two weeks. After I left, I'd more than likely never see him again.

3

Reagan chewed on her bottom lip as she looked over the menu. She looked so damn cute. I wanted to tease her about needing to look at the topping chart at a pizza shop. They were all the same, didn't matter what state you were in – pepperoni was pepperoni. But I didn't. Something had changed when I joked with her in the Jeep, and now she seemed self-conscious.

We ordered, waited for the pizza (in near silence), and we were now back in the Jeep. I'd given her the time she looked like she needed while we were in the restaurant and didn't pry.

Now that we had privacy, all bets were off. I was going to pry. I didn't like the worried look on her face. I don't know why that was, but I didn't.

"What's goin' on?" I asked.

"What do you mean?" She was looking out the passenger window and was worrying her lip again, drawing my attention to their fullness. For a second I'd forgotten what I was going to ask as I wondered if her gloss was the fruity kind. If I kissed her what flavor would I taste?

What. The. Hell? Moving on.

"Let's see, at the gym, you were upbeat and happy. On the way to Jasper's you were quiet and suggested you stay with your parents. After that, you said you didn't want to intrude. Now, you're still quiet and thoughtful. So, what's wrong?"

"Can I ask you something?" she asked, instead of answering.

"Sure." I couldn't promise I would answer, but I left that part out.

"Do you think it's weird I'm here? I mean, it is, right? I'm Liz's sister. The history I have with Jasper. I'm afraid that you all will think I'm some sort of interloper in Emily and Jasper's life. I'm happy for Jasper. I swear I am. He deserves to be happy. I can't wait for him and Emily to get married. Emily's told me how close you all are, and I don't want anyone to think that they have to be nice to me even though they don't want me around. Shit. Forget I said all that. Maybe I should shut up because I think I just made an ass out of myself."

I was in trouble. Big fucking trouble.

In the few hours I'd been around Reagan I'd learned one very important thing about her. She was who she was. How did I know this? Because she let it all hang out. No pretense, no forethought to what she said, she just blurted out whatever came to mind. It didn't matter if we were talking about pizza or her insecurities, she was honest.

I liked that, a whole fuck of a lot.

All of that made her dangerous; that, paired with the way she looked, the way she dressed, and the way she smelled.

I was fucked.

After tonight I had to make myself busy for the next two weeks she was here. Reagan was like Jasper's little sister, and she was young. Ten years younger than me and still wet behind the ears. Just thinking about all the dirty things I wanted to do to her made me feel like a creepy old man.

"Who you are is not a secret. If I'm honest, at first, when I found out you were coming to stay I thought it was a little weird." Reagan's eyes widened, and she started to fidget. "But then I thought about it. Why should it be weird? Take your sister and your niece out of the picture; you and Jasper have been friends for a long time. What happened was horrible. I can't tell you how sorry I am you lost your sister. My brother." I had to stop and take a breath. I couldn't believe I was getting ready to say this. "He died too. I don't think I was as close to him as you were to your sister, but I still know the pain of losing a sibling."

When Reagan came back into focus, there were tears in her eyes. "I'm sorry you lost him. How'd it happen?"

"He was overseas on deployment. His transport helicopter was shot down."

Why the hell was I telling her about Nick? I never talked about him, not even with the team.

"He was in the military too?" she asked.

"Yeah. Army."

She smiled and wiped the corner of her eye. "Sucks doesn't it."

She had no idea. There was a stark difference between the loss of our siblings. The last words I spoke to my brother were in anger after I'd kicked his ass. The worst part, he'd barely fought back. He knew he'd fucked up and deserved the ass kicking. The whole situation was fucked up.

"Yeah, it does."

"Don't worry about what anyone thinks, Reagan. Relax and just be you; they'll love you."

Did I just say, love? When the hell had I started using the word love?

"Thanks for listening."

"Anytime. Let's grab a few twelve packs and get back."

"Do I get to pick the beer since you picked the toppings?" she asked, as I pulled out of the lot.

"Woman, how long does it take to decide what you want on a pizza?"

"Well, you have to decide what combo you want. If you're getting a meat lovers' combo, you don't want to ruin it with veggies. And if you want something healthy you're not going to add extra crumbled sausage."

"That's nutty. You know that, right?"

"Whatever," she mumbled. "What other playlists do you have?"

She didn't wait for me to answer. Instead, she started pushing buttons, going through the stations – finally stopping on a pop station.

"Seriously? You like Ozzy, and you listen to this crap?"

"There is nothing wrong with Maroon 5."

"If you say so. But this shit goes off before we pull back into Jasper's driveway."

I picked out the beer when we went to the liquor store, but only because her mom had called, so she stayed in the Jeep to talk to her while I grabbed what we needed.

On the way back to Jasper's we talked mostly about music as she flipped through my iPod that was connected to the car's stereo system. Bored with my playlists, she turned on satellite radio and stopped back at the pop station. We were debating boy bands; she was trying to tell me that Justin Bieber had one good song, and I was firmly in the position that "good song" and "Justin Bieber" never belonged in the same sentence.

When we rounded the corner turning into Jasper's neighborhood, Reagan started laughing. It started out as a giggle, and by the time we were pulling into Jasper's drive, it was a full-on belly laugh. I couldn't figure out what was so funny.

I noticed Lenox and Levi's trucks were both parked on the street, and I was getting ready to tell her it was time to turn the pop shit off when she turned it up and started singing at the top of her lungs. It was loud, and she smiled at me as she belted out the lyrics. I was momentarily stunned by her playfulness. She looked so sweet and innocent, and my gut twisted in a funny way. Not like when it did when we were on a mission and shit was getting ready to go sideways. It was something else, something far more terrifying. It felt something a lot like happiness. When was the last time I had a woman in my car that was so vibrant, and full of life? She wasn't putting on airs or trying to be sexy. No, not Reagan. Reagan was who she was. I didn't think the girl would know how to play games with a man if someone gave her a playbook.

My hand shot out to turn the god-awful music down before Jasper's neighbors could complain, and she covered the screen so I couldn't turn off the stereo without having to pry her hands away.

Weighing my options, I went with the easiest, which turned out to be the wrong thing to do, and I tickled her until her hand pulled away, uncovering the controls. It was like I was a teenager on my first date and getting my first side-boob feel. Tickling? When the hell had I started tickling, and when did my dick start to stir at the graze of a boob?

"That's not fair," she pouted.

"You're crazy. The neighbors are going to lodge a noise complaint. That shit music should be a violation in itself."

She was nuts, and she was still laughing. If she was so crazy then why did I want to kiss her so badly? I had to get out of the car before I did something stupid, like touch her again. I was slipping further and further into dangerous territory with this girl. Movement over her shoulder caught my attention. Shit. Lenox and Levi were both standing staring at us with their mouths hanging open. Fuck me. I was never going to hear the end of this.

Reagan glanced over her shoulder then back to me.

"Crap. I'm sorry. I didn't know they were out here. God, why am I always embarrassing myself?" Reagan brought both her hands up and covered her face. "Shit. That was so dumb. I can't go out there now."

"Sure, you can. I doubt they even heard the music." There was no way they didn't hear the music, and if by some miracle they didn't, there was no way they missed her bouncing around and singing.

"I can't believe I did that." She was back to laughing. "What am I, fifteen? Seriously, I can't go out and meet them now."

"Come on, Tay-Tay, it's no big deal. The pizza's getting cold."

"Ohmigod, you know her nickname." Reagan laughed. "I knew it. I knew you were a closet Taylor Swift fan."

I wasn't. I hated her music, but I found myself wanting to make her comfortable. I'd examine that later. If Reagan were anyone else jumping around in my Jeep it would've been annoying at best. Yet somehow when she did it, it was funny.

What the hell?

"Yeah, yeah. Keep that to yourself."

I got out, grabbed the pizzas and met Reagan in front of the Jeep. She had a twelve pack in each hand, and it struck me, she didn't even look old enough to drink the beer.

"Here. Let me get those," Levi said as he approached.

Lenox hung back with a thoughtful expression, I knew that look, and honestly – it pissed me off. He was a closet romantic and was going to read more into what had happened in the car. I could handle the guys busting my balls. Hell, I did it to them any chance I could, but I didn't want Lenox to start in with his shit. He thought now that he and Lily were perfectly settled with their little family that everyone should be just as blissfully happy. Then Jasper fell, and now Levi. Lenox was like a badass commando cupid. If I wasn't careful, he'd try and shoot me in the ass and marry me off, something that was never going to happen.

I was happy for my brothers. They'd all found their other halves. Love and marriage weren't for me. I'd tried that once, and it'd left me broken, with a dead brother and cheating bitch for a wife. I'd never do that again, and I was perfectly happy sitting back playing uncle to the rug rats my teammates popped out.

"Thanks. I'm Reagan." She introduced herself before I could.

"Levi," he told her.

"I didn't take you as a teenybopper country music fan," Lenox said when he joined our huddle.

Bastard. Reagan's face turned bright red, and she looked like she was getting ready to bolt.

"There's a lot you don't know about me. Reagan, this is Lenox."

"Seems so," he muttered. There was so much meaning behind those two words. Lenox knew me well. He knew I didn't make a habit of having women in my Jeep, and I certainly didn't smile at them and tickle them as they sang shit music.

"Nice to meet you," Reagan said softly.

Shit, she was red-faced and uncomfortable.

There was no reason for her to be, but after what she'd told me earlier about her being worried about meeting the team, I could see how this was not the first impression she wanted to make. I didn't like seeing her shy and uncertain; this was not her. She should never be embarrassed about who she was – there wasn't a damn thing wrong with her. She had a soft, sweet, vulnerable spot that made me want to wrap her up and protect it; shield it from the world so no one could tarnish it.

Whoa! Where the hell had that come from? I didn't want to protect anyone from anything. I wasn't that guy. Not anymore.

"Pizza's getting cold."

I didn't wait for them to follow before I took off for the door. Warning bells were blaring all over the place. I needed a minute away from her to get my head on straight. She was too much. Too pretty. Too sweet. Too goddamned perfect.

4

Crap!

I did it again.

I swear that was the running theme song of my life. Maybe I should change my name to Britney, shave my head, and stop wearing panties. That might've been less embarrassing. I couldn't stop making a fool of myself, and to make matters worse, this time I'd done it in front of Jasper's friends. Clark was bad enough, but Lenox and Levi too.

Sweet Jesus, I wish a hole would open up and swallow me whole.

"Come on Madonna, let's get you in the house," Levi laughed.

I groaned, Lenox laughed, and Clark growled. At least that's what I thought he'd done. He'd stomped off after he'd irately declared the pizza was getting cold. Not that I could blame him; I'd acted like a twelve-year-old in his car and undoubtedly annoyed the hell out of him. I'm sure the women he was used to would never blast Taylor Swift and behave like an immature teenager.

When we walked into the house, the noise level hit me first. Jason was playing with a toddler on the living room floor. The baby, who had to be Carter, Lenox and Lily's son, was banging on a toy and laughing. Emily was in the kitchen with two other women, each had a glass of wine in their hands, and they were laughing. I was happy to see that Emily's friends were able to put a smile on her face after the news she got today.

Clark had put the pizzas on the dining room table, and I caught sight of him as he closed the sliding door to the backyard. Jason's German Shepherd puppy came bouncing up to Clark, jumping wildly around his feet. Clark didn't pay attention to the puppy and disappeared around the corner.

Crap.

He was mad at me. I needed to apologize then avoid him the rest of the time I was here. Before I could follow Clark and probably make more of a fool of myself, Emily thankfully stopped me.

"Reagan. Come meet the girls."

I tried to breathe and calm my nerves as I walked to the women. "Hi."

"I'm Blake," the pretty brown-haired woman said.

"I'm Lily. We're so happy you're finally here. Emily has been so excited to have you visit. How long are you staying?" Lily asked.

Wow, these women were gorgeous. Not that I'd expected anything else after meeting their husbands outside.

"I'm not sure, I was planning on two weeks, but I might have to cut it short a little," I answered.

"What? Why?" Emily asked.

"My mom called and is grumbling about me visiting with them for a few days before I start my new job."

That was a partial truth. My mom did want me to come and stay, but the bigger reason was I didn't think I belonged here. Then there was Clark. My brain didn't work around him, and all I seemed to do was make him mad.

"Well, that's too bad. But you know moms. Mine drives me crazy and insists on weekly visits," Emily laughed.

Something passed across Lily's face, sadness

maybe. But whatever it was, it made me want to change the subject.

"Anyway, I need to get unpacked and get my place in order before I start my new job."

"What do you do?" Blake asked.

"I'm in PR and advertising. I got a job with a new start-up. They landed their first big client and are eager to start."

"That sounds fun. Maybe we'll see your work on TV or something," Lily added.

"Doubtful. It's not as glamorous as one would think. The new client is an oil company. They've run into some environmentalists that have smeared their name. They're trying to rebrand themselves as eco-friendly," I explained.

"Good luck pulling that off. Lots of people want the oil companies to stop drilling off the coast, especially after the recent spills," Blake said.

"I know it's going to be a nightmare, that's why they're so eager to start. Two of their rigs are off-line, there are too many protesters surrounding the platform. They can't even get the boats off the docks to take the workers out to the drill."

"Who's hungry?" Lenox asked, cutting off our conversation.

"Me," Jason yelled and ran into the kitchen. "Pizza's my favorite. Did Uncle Clark get me a slice of meat lovers?"

"He did, bud," I told him.

"Righteous," Jason yelled again, and fist bumped the air.

The room laughed at his very adult comment, Levi stopping first and turning his gaze on me. Oh no, I didn't like that look.

"So, you thinking of putting on an encore performance?"

The women looked at him, not understanding what he was talking about, and Lenox very helpfully filled them in. Soon the whole room had erupted in laughter. My humiliation was complete.

"Hey," Lily whispered beside me. She, too, had been laughing at me. "They're not making fun of you. No one would be laughing and joking with you if you weren't part of the group. This is just Levi's way to include you. It means you're one of us."

I didn't understand how making fun of me made me one of them, but I didn't think Lily would lie to me. Maybe I was being a baby. It didn't bother me when my friends laughed at my antics, why should I let it bother me now? Because I was trying to impress them and make them like me. Clark had told me to be myself; that sounded like solid advice. I had to get over myself and stop worrying so much.

"What did Clark do?" Jasper asked through his laughter.

"I couldn't get a lock, but it looked like he tickled her until she finally moved and he could turn down Taylor Swift and make little miss superstar stop singing." Levi good-naturedly explained. "Maybe you'll take requests next time. Something that is passable as music."

I had a good comeback ready when my words died in my throat. Clark had come back into the house, and he was currently engaged in a stare down with Jasper.

Shit. Shit. Damn.

The puppy ran into the house behind Clark and beelined it to Carter on the floor. No one else seemed to notice, so I moved to pick up the toddler as Rambo (yes, Jason named the dog Rambo) licked Carter's face. Not that the kid minded; he was screeching and laughing at the exuberant puppy.

I sneezed loudly, not able to stifle it fast enough and Carter belted out a cry.

"I'm sorry, baby. I didn't mean to scare you." I nuzzled my face into his neck and blew a raspberry. Carter giggled, and I did it again. "You think that's funny, huh?" I continued to tickle Carter, enjoying his baby smell and sweet laugh. "You're a cute little thing. Bet your mama's gonna lock you away from all those crazy girls." Carter grabbed my face and planted a big wet kiss on my lips. "Easy there, tiger, I'm a little old for you." I was rubbing my nose against his, giving him Eskimo kisses, when I noticed the room had gone silent.

"I'm sorry. I should've asked before I picked him up. Rambo was licking him. I'm sorry - here." I tried to pass Carter off to Lily, but she stepped back not taking the baby.

"Don't be silly. You don't have to ask to pick him up," Lenox said.

"He doesn't go to strangers. Ever. He cries when anyone new gets near him," Lily added. "He likes you."

With the weight of everyone's stares I felt oddly on display and vulnerable; so I did what I do best and made an ass out of myself.

"It's my charming personality. The boys can't help themselves around me." I turned back to Carter and nuzzled him again. "Huh? You can't help but fall in love and kiss me." Carter laughed and smacked both my cheeks – hard. "Whoa there, commando baby, gentle."

Lenox nearly busted a gut he laughed so hard. "I like her."

After that, no one seemed to pay attention to me as they served up the pizza and started eating. No one except Clark that is. He still looked angry with me. I wanted to talk to him, but I didn't. I avoided him the rest of the night. If he entered the kitchen, I exited. When he and the guys went out back, I made sure to stay in the house with the girls.

By the end of the night, I felt comfortable with all of them. They were every bit as awesome as Emily had said. Blake was a badass like the guys. She wasn't in the Army but worked with them. No one had given specifics, but I figured out she gathered intelligence. Up until recently, she lived in DC, only moving to Georgia and marrying Levi a few weeks ago.

The guys were funny once I got over them poking fun at me any chance they got. Well, Jasper, Levi, and Lenox did. Clark hadn't talked to me.

"You look like shit," Jasper said when he and the guys came back into the house.

"Thanks. You're so kind."

"Your eyes are red and puffy," he said.

"And she's been sneezing like crazy," Emily put in.

"Are you allergic to dogs?" Lily asked.

"I don't think so. We never had a dog growing up, but I've been around them before obviously," I answered.

"Every time Rambo gets near you is when you sneeze," Blake offered.

"Well damn. Maybe it's just the pollen down here." It was Rambo; I knew it was. I was just hoping no one had noticed and I didn't know my eyes had turned red. I didn't want Emily and Jasper to worry about the dog and me. They had been cool to offer to let me stay with them, and I didn't want to be a pain in the ass.

"We can keep him outside," Jasper said.

"No way. That's not fair to the puppy. Besides, you are trying to house train him. If you make him stay in the backyard, he won't learn. I'll be fine."

Rambo came running over as if he knew we were talking about him and I tried to cover up my sneeze with a cough.

Multiple things happened at once.

"The dog goes out," Emily demanded.

"She can stay with us. We just painted the spare room for the baby, so the window has to stay open," Lenox offered.

"She can have the couch at our house," Levi said.

"She'll stay with me. She's not sleeping on a couch. And it's humid as balls out; no way is anyone sleeping with a window open. Rambo would bark his head off if you lock him outside and no one would get rest for a three-mile radius with a puppy yapping all night."

Then they all agreed with Clark; "you're right" "it's settled" and "good idea" filled the room as I sat in shock.

I was not staying with Clark. I wasn't some kid that needed the adults in the room to make sleeping arrangements for her. I could stay in a hotel for the night, or I could take some allergy medication and tough it out.

"You ready?" Lenox asked Lily.

"Yeah, Carter is wiped."

And that started off the "goodbyes" and "nice to meet yous." It was a good thing everyone else was leaving. I could tell Jasper and Emily I was going to a hotel without an audience. Clark would be there, but he no longer counted as a stranger to me. Besides, I needed to talk to him too.

"Listen, guys; I'm fine really."

I wasn't done with the speech I had prepared about how tough I was, and a little dog wasn't going to bother me when Clark cut me off.

"You're not fine. Your eyes are puffy, you've been sneezing, and now your nose is starting to run."

"Thanks for pointing all that out, Captain Obvious," I snapped.

I didn't like that Clark was seeing me like this. I still hadn't looked in the mirror, but I was sure I looked like shit. I wasn't vain, but I still didn't want to look miserable in front of the man. He was freaking model gorgeous. Here I was thinking about ripping off his clothes every time I looked at him and having my way with him, and he was thinking about getting me a Kleenex for my runny nose.

Why me?

"Rea, I think it's a good idea you stay with Clark. If you stay here, loaded up on allergy meds, you'll be groggy and miserable," Jasper said.

"Besides, you don't want your eyes all bloodshot for the wedding pictures," Emily added.

I was beginning to annoy myself for being so insecure, but maybe this was the out they wanted. Both seemed very happy for me to be leaving their home. I could make it easier for everyone and leave with Clark. He'd understand once I explained to him why I needed to stay in a hotel. Well, mostly he'd understand the excuses I was going to offer. I would not, however, be telling him the whole truth. That was too embarrassing.

"Okay. I'll pack up my stuff now."

I didn't have a lot to clean up and shove in my suitcase. I spent the time preparing what I was going to say to Clark.

Staying with him wasn't an option. There was no way I could be around the man without doing something stupid like begging him to kiss me, or better yet, pleading with him to touch me. While I was at it, knowing me, I'd probably admit that I've never had an orgasm and ask him to give me one of those too. Yep, that was something I'd totally do, then Clark would run a mile and kick my ass out on the street.

Huh, maybe that wasn't such a bad idea. That might have to be my backup plan.

5

_____

I'd spent the silence of the drive over to my place trying to figure out when I'd turned into such a dumbass. It was no wonder Levi, Jasper, and Lenox all had looked at me like I'd grown three heads when I offered for Reagan to stay at my house. The women had readily agreed and wouldn't understand the significance of my offer. But the guys did, and Jasper had eyed me until he finally relented and nodded his approval.

Now I was fucked. Stuck in the middle of a rock and a hard place not sure how to proceed, which was unusual for me. I normally knew with great clarity my plan of attack. Only with her, I couldn't seem to get my head on straight. My thoughts and feelings about her seemed to be as clear as mud. I didn't want to be around her, but I didn't want her out of my sight. Thankfully none of the guys had asked or brought up Reagan when we were out back. The team had bigger things to worry about than a girl singing in my Jeep. We had new information about an oil platform owned by Alger Energy. After months of digging and gathering intel, Blake thought she'd finally put together the pieces and wanted to meet tomorrow at the hangar to go over details.

Reagan seemed to be thinking as well and made no effort to make small talk or fuss with the radio. I should've been grateful for the silence, but I found I didn't like it, not with her. So much of my life was chaotic; I normally liked the solitude and stillness. I didn't need mindless chatter to fill the void. But with her sitting next to me it felt wrong, lonely even. She was a few feet away from me, but we might as well have been miles.

Why wasn't I happy she didn't want to talk?

We pulled up to the house I rented, and I wondered if she'd be scared way out in the middle of nowhere with me. I should've told her I lived off the beaten path. My closest neighbor was miles away, just how I liked it. No one to bother me.

"This is beautiful," she said, putting my fears to rest. "Back home in Montana, before my parents moved, we had five hundred acres. Dad rented it out to a rancher who raised beef cattle."

I had forgotten she'd grown up in the country; so much of her screamed city girl.

"I like it out here, reminds me of home too."

"Where are you from?" she asked.

"Nebraska. Come on, let's get inside," I suggested before she could ask me anything more. And for the first time in my adult life, it wasn't because I didn't want a woman prying into my life, but because I was finding I didn't mind telling her things. And that bothered me.

I left her by the front door and went to disarm the alarm and turn on lights.

"Wow. This is really nice," she said. "Not what I expected."

"What'd you expect? A shithole?" I laughed, this girl just blurted out the first thing she thought, social grace be damned.

"No. I guess I expected more of a bachelor pad. You know gun racks, swords mounted on the walls, posters of naked women." She smiled. "I'm joking, by the way."

"I've lived most of my life holed up in dirty, shit places. When I'm home, I want to be around nice things."

"I thought you guys tested gear and stuff. Mostly paperwork. Did you deploy a lot before you came to Georgia?"

I was getting too comfortable around her and forgetting myself.

"Yeah. Something like that. Come on; I'll show you to your room."

She quietly followed me down the hall, stopping behind me when I pushed the door open to the spare bedroom and stepped aside.

"The bathroom is across the hall. There are towels in the linen closet in there. I don't have girly shit, but there's soap under there too. "

"Thanks, Clark. I appreciate you letting me stay here. I'll look for a hotel to stay in tomorrow."

"Why would you do that? You can stay here until you go to Florida."

Why did I just offer that? If she wanted to stay in a hotel, I should be ecstatic and offer to help her find one.

"For one, I don't want to put you out. It's cool of you to let me crash here tonight. I got the impression that both Jasper and Emily were happy to have me go. They nearly pushed me out the door with you. The truth is, I'm gonna head down to Florida soon anyway. I'll fly up for the wedding if they still want me there."

"That's fucked."

"What is?" she asked.

"That you think so little of Emily and Jasper that you'd say they were pushing you out of their house. I was standing there; that's not what happened. The fact you'd even say that is more about you than them. I watched everyone tonight; they all welcomed you into the fold. Even Levi, and I gotta tell you that is surprising. His trust issues make mine look normal."

"You have trust issues?" she asked.

I didn't know what to do with this woman; she had no sense of margins whatsoever.

"Reagan," I snapped.

"You're right. It does say something about me. It says I'm a self-absorbed bitch that is more worried about my feelings than the kindness that others have shown me. And before you say it, I know, I need to get the fuck over myself. But I don't know how to do it. I'm scared. I know it sounds stupid, but I lost Jasper's friendship for a long time. And it sucked, big time. He was always my big brother, a part of my family. I'm waiting for that to get ripped away again. Did you know when I was growing up, Jasper was the one I cried to when a boy broke my heart or the girls in school were acting like stuck-up bitches? And that was often. I had my sister and Jasper. That was it. Then everything happened with Liz, and he disappeared and left us. When they died, all I wished for was for him to be there. He'd know what to do; he would handle everything. My mom was a mess, my dad was completely shattered, and I didn't have the first clue how to fix it. But he would've. If I lose that again, it's gonna suck."

I was pissed, and I didn't understand why, and I couldn't wrap my head around the irrational jealousy that was pushing its way out of my mouth. "Are you in love with him?"

Reagan stumbled back like I'd physically struck her. "What the hell did you just ask me?"

"Kinda sounds like it."

"Did you miss the part where I said he was a big brother to me. I have never looked at Jasper in a way that was not brotherly, ever. First, he belonged to my sister, and there are lines you do not cross in this world. Touching, thinking about, or stealing your sister's boyfriend is on the top of the list. I loved my sister and would never in a million years think about touching her man. Even after they'd broken up. He has always been my friend. Just a friend. You know what those are, right? Someone you can count on and talk to. Someone that will hold your hand through shit times. That's all he's ever been and will be to me. I want Jasper happy. Emily is the person that can give him the life he deserves. Her and Jason. He needs to be a father." Reagan stopped, and she cut her eyes at me; even fuming mad and red-eyed she was gorgeous. "And fuck you for thinking I was the type of woman that would break up a family."

I deserved that.

However, she had it all wrong. I wasn't accusing her; I was envious. Only I couldn't explain that to her without telling her I was consumed with jealousy when she spoke about Jasper and their friendship. I didn't want to tell her that not all siblings had those same boundaries and they would fuck your wife while you were on deployment.

For some unknown reason, I wanted to be the person she wanted around when she needed someone. That thought freaked me the fuck out. Why in God's good name would I ever want the responsibility of another woman? Especially knowing, in the end, they always screwed you over. But not Reagan. I knew down to my soul she wouldn't lie to and cheat on her man.

"I'm sorry. I shouldn't have said that. That's not how I meant it."

"Oh no? Then how'd you mean it?"

This girl was feisty. I couldn't remember another time that a woman had held my feet to the fire and didn't let me off the hook. My wife never did. She either didn't care enough, or she was too busy chasing Nick to worry about what I was doing.

"I didn't mean it to come out sounding like I thought you'd go after Jasper. Not then and not now."

"Then why'd you say it?" she demanded, not relenting.

"Just take my word -"

"Seriously? You call me a homewrecker and you want me to take your word?"

"I said it because I was fucking jealous hearing you talk about Jasper like that. There - are you happy now?"

Good god, she was pushy.

"What?" she whispered.

"Time for bed Reagan. I'll see you in the morning."

Instead of heading straight to bed I went outside. I needed a drink and a cigarette to calm my nerves and try to settle my racing thoughts.

Since when did I allow a woman to push me into

saying more than I wanted? How in the hell did she get me to admit I was jealous?

Shit.

"Sorry to interrupt." She was screwing with my head so bad I hadn't heard the back door open. "I wanted to apologize."

"Nothing to apologize for."

"There is. I embarrassed you earlier with my childish behavior and just now for being overly sensitive. If I said I'd overreacted, it'd be an understatement. I'm nervous, and when that happens, I tend not to think before I speak. I'd like to say it won't happen again, but I'm sure it will."

How was that for honest?

"Rea, you didn't embarrass me earlier."

I regretted the use of her nickname as soon as it slipped out of my mouth. Calling her that seemed far too familiar, and I was trying to keep some distance between us.

"Then why'd you get all broody and stomp away. Not to mention you gave yourself a timeout and went outside as soon as we got there."

This girl was too fucking much. I took a long pull from my cigarette wishing I was alone to enjoy the one smoke a day I allowed myself in peace. "I just needed a minute to myself."

"Okay. Well, goodnight Clark." She looked so dejected, and for once she didn't push. I should've stopped her and explained further, but I didn't. I needed time to think.

"Goodnight Reagan."

After Reagan left me outside, I finished my cigarette and went to bed; tossing and turning into the early dawn hours. I couldn't still my mind or my body. I laid there for hours trying to figure out why I had such a strong reaction to a woman that I barely knew. The physical attraction was a no-brainer. The girl was smokin' hot. But the emotional connection? That made absolutely no sense.

6

Something had pulled me from a fitful sleep. It took a moment for me to get my bearings and remember I was in Clark's guest room. I sat up in bed and listened, but there was nothing but silence. Just as I dismissed the noise as a dream, I heard it again. It sounded like a man yelling. Without thought, I quickly got out of bed and went to the door. Stopping to listen before I left the safety of my room, I heard it again. Clark yelled out again, but I didn't hear anyone else. Maybe he was on the phone at - I glanced at the alarm clock on the dresser – four am.

What the hell?

I moved down the hallway toward his bedroom and heard it again.

"Get the fuck off of him," Clark yelled.

I held my breath, waiting to hear someone else's voice or commotion in the room. Nothing. His plea was met with silence.

I tapped on the door and waited.

"I will fucking kill you," he growled.

This time it sounded like there was bang on the wall to accompany his shout.

"Just shoot me and end this."

I waited another few seconds and braved opening his door.

It was wrong and intrusive, and I didn't give two shits. Something was wrong.

"Shoot me, motherfucker. We both know you're going to."

Clark was in bed thrashing around. His bed sheet was tangled around his legs getting more so as he kicked his feet out and twisted his torso. His face was awash with agony, and his fists were balled at his sides. The closer I got to the bed the more I could see. Even in the early morning light, I could make out the sweat beading on his forehead, rolling down the bridge of his nose and mixing with his tears.

There was something so wrong seeing this big strong man in the grips of a nightmare. He looked tortured, and I couldn't stand for it another minute. With two more strides, I made it to the side of his bed and leaned over him, shaking him as hard as I could.

"Wake up, Clark."

Nothing. He thrashed back and forth, and I tried again.

"Clark," I yelled this time.

One minute I was shaking him; the next we'd crashed to the floor. Clark landed on top of me pushing all the air out of my lungs.

"Ouch! Clark! Wake up." I struggled against his hold, but I couldn't move; he was too heavy.

When I finally focused in the dim light, I wished I hadn't. Clark was staring down at me, his face twisted in anger. His eyes were so full of hate that even though I'd just had the wind knocked out of me, this was somehow more. It was hard to breathe, and it had nothing to do with Clark's body weight pressing me to the floor. His expression, while furious, was also somehow dead. He wasn't looking at me; he was looking through me to another place and time.

"Clark, please, you're hurting me. Wake up." I stopped fighting and laid limp under him and tried again. "It's me, Reagan. You're hurting me. You're in your room - safe. Please wake up."

He slowly blinked his eyes and they snapped to

mine. "No one is going to hurt you. You're safe in your house in Georgia." The more I softly spoke to him, the more alert he became.

"Reagan?" he whispered.

"Yeah, it's me. You awake yet?" I asked.

Instead of relaxing as I hoped, his body stiffened, and his muscles in his chest flexed. "What the fuck," he barked and pinned my hands.

"Please wake up," I cried.

"I am." He released my hands and rolled to the side, shifted, and brought me up to a sitting position still on the floor. "What the hell were you thinking touching me?"

I was stunned and pissed. What the hell was his problem?

"You were having a nightmare; I tried to wake you up."

I tried to push up to stand, but Clark grabbed hold of me and pulled me into his lap. His skin was hot and dewy, and tear tracks coated his cheeks.

"I hurt you," he surmised, the grief no longer from what had tortured him in his sleep.

"No, you didn't."

"Then why are you crying?" he asked and wiped the tears from my face.

How did I explain to him without making the

situation worse? If he knew how scared I'd been, he'd be horrified.

"You startled me is all. I didn't expect you to react the way you did. But you didn't hurt me. I'm fine. I shouldn't have come in here. It was an invasion of your privacy."

His thumb stilled on my cheek, and he gripped my face. Even in the screwed-up situation when he looked into my eyes while holding my cheek, sweaty for the horror he'd dreamt, I wanted to kiss him. This wasn't anything new. I'd wanted to put my lips on his since the moment I'd seen him, but this was different. I wanted to comfort him, soothe his tortured soul, bring him back to the here and now. As odd as it was seeing Clark crumpled on the floor, vulnerable, it was... sexy. It made him seem more approachable, more human.

"You shouldn't be in here. I'm dangerous."

He was more correct than he knew. He was dangerous - to my health. My mental health to be exact. He was undoubtedly going to be my biggest regret. Clark had heartbreaker written all over him. No, scratch that, *heartbreaker* was a huge flashing neon sign above his head. I knew it, I saw it, and it was too late. It didn't matter which way I went from here on out; I was screwed. And at the moment I was leaning towards taking the coward's way and running.

"Reagan?" he asked.

"Huh? Sorry."

"I was saying, you shouldn't be in here," he repeated.

"You didn't hurt me." I tried to reassure him, but he shook his head. "You wanna talk about it?"

"It's nothing for you to worry about."

"I didn't ask that. I asked if you wanted to talk about it. Why don't you let me worry about what I should and shouldn't worry about?"

Clark was quiet for a long time. Long enough for me to wiggle in his lap to try and get the blood flowing back to my tingling butt cheeks.

My movement must've pulled him from his contemplation and, to my surprise, he began. "My team was on a low-risk reconnaissance mission. I knew the minute we hit the ground something was off. My gut was screaming at me to turn back and scrap the op. My second in command felt it too. I was getting ready to tell my men to fall back when the man we were sent in to get intel on suddenly appeared. We continued with the mission. By the time I saw that it was a setup, it was too late. My team was almost surrounded. I gave the order to scatter. All but one obeyed my call. My second stayed behind to provide the rest of the team cover as they fell back. He wouldn't leave. He disobeyed a direct order. The more I argued with him to leave, the more resolute he was that he wouldn't leave my six. We were captured." Clark looked like he'd gone into a trance as he told me his story. His tone was flat and haunting. "We were held for five days before a CAG team could come in and rescue us. By then it was too late, Moses was already dead."

"I'm so sorry." My words sounded lame even to my own ears, but there was nothing else I could say.

"He had a baby back home he'd never met. All he had to do was follow my fucking orders." I didn't know what to say, so I remained quiet. "Fuck."

"How long ago?"

"Ten years. Can you believe I still have nightmares ten years later?" Clark shook his head, then slammed it back against the side of the mattress. "Weak."

"You are not weak. Don't ever say that," I scolded. "What's a CAG team?"

"What?" Clark asked, his eyes widening.

"You said a CAG team rescued you." I reminded him, not understanding why his voice had hardened.

"It's a Combat Applications Group," he answered.

"Nope, still lost. I don't know what that is."

On an exhale he shifted. "Let's get off the floor."

We stood, and I noticed for the first time since we'd landed on the floor that Clark only wore a pair of tight boxer briefs.

Holy shit. The outline of his dick was clearly visible under the white cotton. The light coming in from the windows was giving the room just enough illumination to appreciate the bulge, and as if on cue, his dick twitched, causing me to jerk my eyes away and straight into Clark's hot gaze. Well shit, I'd been caught, so I might as well continue my perusal. His chest was bare, showcasing his tattoos. I wanted to see them up close, but I dared not move, afraid I wouldn't be able to resist reaching out and tracing the lines. He had several marks on his lower abdomen; they were nearly camouflaged between the lines of his eight-pack - I counted the hard ridges. My eyes drifted further down glancing at the swelling between his legs. I wasn't well-versed in male anatomy, but in my very limited experience, even I knew his package was abnormally large. I wanted to get a closer look at that, too.

"Don't lick your lips," Clark groaned.

"What?" I stepped back from him.

"Don't lick your lips while checking out my cock, Rea," he semi repeated.

"I...I hadn't realized I did," I stammered out. Crap, how embarrassing.

"Well, you did."

I chanced a look at him, and the heat on my cheeks intensified. He'd crossed his arms over his chest (sadly covering his pectoral muscles from my view) and wore a smug look on his handsome face. He really was too good-looking for his own good. I wondered how many women had fallen for that sexy smirk and broad chest. Probably a lot. More than I cared to think about, but enough to know he was way-*way* - out of my league. I had seen exactly two men fully naked, well in person - I'd seen plenty of others on the internet. Neither of the men had the muscles that Clark had or the promise of what he was packing under those boxers of his. Christ almighty, I bet he'd never had issues making his women orgasm. Hell, just thinking about what he could do to me made my panties dampen and my girly parts clench. That was new. I'd been turned on before but never have I had an overwhelming urge to throw a man down and finally find out what all the fuss was about sex.

Clark cleared his throat, pulling me (once again) from my thoughts. "Sorry. I'll let you get back to sleep, or whatever it is you do in the morning." I had to get away from him before I said something I'd regret. "Sorry again for the intrusion."

7

"You hungry?" I asked Reagan before she could flee.

"What?" She turned back around, the blush that had graced her pretty face had now spread down to her neck, and I wanted to know if it also extended further down to her breasts.

"Well, since you keep licking your sexy as fuck lips, I thought maybe you were hungry."

Her eyes narrowed on me, but she didn't move - which was a pity. I'd hoped she'd cross her arms over her chest so the t-shirt she was wearing would ride up and I could ascertain if she had shorts on under the long hem or if she was only wearing panties. I was seriously hoping for just panties. Sometime between tossing and turning last night, thinking about Reagan, and her trying to comfort me after my nightmare about Moses (even though I knew she was scared as fuck) I'd decided I wasn't going to fight the attraction between us. I was going to have to be very careful because of her friendship with Jasper, but we were both adults. There was no reason we shouldn't explore each other for long hours in my bed - and on every available surface of my house. I'd have to fully explain that I wasn't capable of giving her more than a few days and a shit ton of orgasms, not that she'd want more than that. She didn't even live in Georgia and would be gone within two weeks, if not sooner from what she'd said last night.

"I didn't mean to," she whispered.

Reagan wasn't playing coy, that wasn't her style. She normally blurted out whatever she was thinking. She really had no idea how sexy she was, or that her little pink tongue had brushed her bottom lip, leaving it wet and glistening in its wake. The sight conjured up thoughts of her pussy. Was it wet and as slippery as her lip looked? Fuck, I wanted, no, *needed* to know.

She backed up as I moved toward her, the annoyance turning into shock. I liked that look. It was refreshing having a woman react naturally. When her back hit the door, I placed my hands on the wood over her shoulders, caging her in, but careful not to touch her.

"What part didn't you mean to do?" I asked, trying my hardest to ignore my throbbing hard-on.

"I don't understand your question." Her voice was soft and unsure. Her eyes darted around, not landing on any part of my body for too long.

"What part, Reagan, did you not mean to do? Stare at my cock until it was hard enough to pound nails? Or draw my attention to your mouth, making me lose my mind wondering what it would be like to lick that lip for you? Or what it would feel like to have your tongue glide over my cock that way?"

"You thought that?" she asked.

If I had any other woman pressed up against my bedroom door, I would've rolled my eyes and known she was running a play – shy and innocent. But there was no hiding the disbelief in Reagan's voice.

Without being able to stop myself, I pressed my lower half against her stomach and flexed my hips. When her eyes snapped to mine, I was satisfied she knew I was telling the truth about my erection. I pulled back a fraction but still kept us touching.

"Holy crap," she mumbled.

That was not the reaction I was expecting, though I should've with Reagan. Her lack of response made me second guess myself. Did I misread her interest? Most other women would've touched me by now, grabbed onto what I had offered.

I eased back a little further when her words cut through my doubt and rocked my world.

"I, um, don't know what I'm supposed to do here. I mean, I'm not a virgin, but I've never done this..."

"Done what, sweets?" I asked.

"Well... I've never been pressed up against a door - turned on - before. I've only seen two men naked in real life and I know I didn't stare at their penises or want to touch them or lick my lips when I looked at them. I don't know if I'm reading this right. I'm not trying to be dumb, I know it sounds stupid but does a man's penis get hard like that because someone stares at it? It doesn't, right? That'd be crazy, that would mean that every time a woman looks at your crotch in public you'd get a stiffy."

I regretted the bark of laughter as soon as it escaped. Reagan's body locked tight, and she flinched. "Don't laugh at me," she whispered.

"I'm not laughing at you, I promise. I'm laughing because you're cute as hell. You don't hold shit back, and I love that about you. There is no guessing what you are thinking or feeling, no hiding and playing games. What you see is what you get. And Rea, I have to tell you that is a huge turn-on for me. So, to answer your questions; no, my cock doesn't get hard when someone looks at it. It gets hard when a sexy, beautiful woman is standing in front of me in nothing but a tee, and she is looking at my cock like she wants to devour it. My male ego likes that you've never been pressed up against a door. But I'll be as honest with you as you were with me. I want you, Reagan. I want nothing more than to spread you out and feast on every inch of you. But I need you to know I'm not looking for a relationship. I'm not boyfriend material. I can offer you one thing, orgasms. Nothing more."

"I've never had one of those," she blurted.

"One of what?"

"An orgasm."

It was my turn to stare at her in shock. "Never?"

"Ohmygod I can't believe I just said that to you." She tried to bring her hands up, presumably to cover her face, but I intercepted them and held them between us.

"So, you have?" I asked needing clarification.

"No, I haven't. I just can't believe what an idiot I am saying that to you."

With the information Reagan had shared, we needed a new venue and a much-needed conversation. I couldn't concentrate with my cock pressed against her belly and her fresh floral scent surrounding me.

"Why don't we go out into the kitchen and I'll make us some coffee?" I asked, dropping her hands.

"No, no, that's okay. I'll go into my room and let you start your day. I don't want to be in your way."

Her head was bowed, shoulders slumped forward, and she'd closed down.

"Look at me." I lifted her chin, forcing her gaze up. "What's wrong?"

"Umm... nothing. I just don't want to bother you. You've been really cool letting me stay here and not mad that I came into your room uninvited."

"Reagan, don't do that. Don't start hiding from me. And as far as the invitation, you're invited into my room whenever you want." I winked at her, hoping to assuage whatever was bothering her.

"Listen, I get it. I ruined the moment announcing my sexual status or lack thereof. Whatever you want to call it. I told you, I've never done any of this, I don't know how to be sexy and all that. You don't have to feel obligated to make me coffee to make me feel better because I'm a complete jackass."

"Stop doing that. You're not an idiot or a jackass. You don't have to try and be sexy, you just are. I give zero fucks about your lack of sexual experience. Well, that's a lie, I do care. The thought of being the man to give you your first orgasm makes me want to pound my chest and simultaneously lie you on my bed and get to work. But before that happens, I need to slow this down and talk. You are not some chick I just met. First, you are friends with Jasper, and he is one of my best friends. I won't do anything that would jeopardize our friendship. Secondly, I have come to care about you as a friend, and I need to make sure before I take us there..." I stopped and gestured to the bed. "We're on the same page. I can't do that when my cock is so close to your pussy I can feel the heat radiating through your panties. Not to mention I'm dying to see for myself if you're as wet as I think you are."

"So why don't you check?" she shyly asked.

"Because if my hand goes anywhere near you, I won't be able to stop." I leaned in and finally did what I've been dying to do since I'd first met her. The first brush of my tongue against her full bottom lip caused my cock to once again harden. Before she could open her mouth, I moved to her neck, noting the scent of lilac or lavender was stronger there. I placed a few light kisses there, and she tilted her head, giving me more room to explore her soft skin.

When I got to the barely exposed flesh of her collarbone and licked the area above the neckline of her tee, she moaned and pressed into me.

I was in trouble, in way too deep with this girl. I knew it and still couldn't stop it. I was going to have her. I'd deal with the fallout when the time came. I knew I couldn't keep her and as long as she walked away unhurt, I'd take the memory of her and tuck it away, secure in the knowledge I'd tasted heaven once in my lifetime.

I sucked and kissed and nibbled around her neck, and when I knew that I was close to exploding in my boxers without her even touching me, I pulled back, happy when I saw her face relaxed and the ever-present blush on her cheeks still there.

"You ready for some coffee so we can talk?" I asked, my lips still on her skin.

"No. I don't want coffee. I want you to touch me."

"We need to talk first," I told her.

"No, we don't. I get it, you're not looking for anything serious, and neither am I. I live in Florida, you live here. I'll probably never see you again after I leave so you don't have to worry about me thinking you're offering me a white picket fence and all that. I just want you to touch me."

The thought of never seeing her again made my gut clench, and suddenly a white picket fence didn't seem so bad.

What in the actual fuck?

Shaking the crazy, asinine image from my head, I reached for her hand without removing my mouth from the crook of her neck. Finding her hand flat against the door, I took it in mine and brought it to my chest, covering her small hand with mine.

"Are you sure? I don't want to hurt you, Rea. I need to know you are a hundred percent on board with what is about to happen."

"I'm positive Clark."

"Nolan."

"What?" she asked.

"My name is Nolan. My last name is Clark."

I don't know why I told her my first name. No one ever called me Nolan. I haven't introduced myself or given my first name to a woman in ten years. I hated to be called Nolan. The only person that calls me that is Moses' wife when I make my monthly calls to check on her and Nathan. Other than that, I hear it in my nightmares enough as Moses is bleeding out, pleading with me to take care of his family for him. *Nolan, they're everything to me. Tell Mari I love her. I loved her and our baby to my*

dying breath just like I promised her I would. Nolan,
please don't forget, promise me you'll tell her.

"Hey, where'd you go?" Reagan asked, pulling
me from my memory. Her small, soft hand flexing
under mine.

"Nowhere, sorry."

"So, your name is Nolan, huh." She smiled and
with more force moved her hand from under mine,
gently using her thumb to graze my skin.

Fuck, her hand felt so good on me. I wanted
more.

"I want you to touch me. Above the waist." I
quickly added. There was no chance I'd be able to
control myself if her hand wrapped around my cock.

"I want to touch you lower," she told me as her
hands traveled up and down my abdomen, her
fingers stopping just above the waistband of my
boxers.

"No. If you touch me, my thinly leashed control
will snap, and you'll be bent over my bed in two
point five seconds."

"Maybe I want to be bent over your bed."

She was killing me, absolutely killing me. I
grabbed her hand just as the tips of her fingers made
their way under the elastic band.

"No, Reagan. I'm not going to fuck you, but I'm

going to make you come on my fingers. Then we are going to go in the living room, have a conversation, and if you still want to proceed, I'm going to bring you back in here and eat you until you come in my mouth. After that, we'll shower, and you can use the rest of the day to decide how far you want to take this."

Shower? Did I just tell her we were going to shower? Together? What the hell was it about this woman that made me lose my mind?

"What about you? Do I get to return the favor?"

Time to move this along. Once the edge was off and she was thinking clearly without the sexual fog clouding her judgment, she'd put a stop to this. We'd drink some coffee, retreat to our own rooms, and I'd take a shower – alone – and jerk off thinking about fingering her.

"Keep your hands above my waist," I growled. "Tell me, Rea. Are you wearing shorts under this tee or just panties?"

"Just panties," she squeaked and shifted, bringing her feet closer together.

I sucked on her neck and pulled the hem of her shirt up, making sure I touched her flesh as I slowly pulled it up. When I broke the suction to rip the shirt over her head, I lost her hands on my skin but gained so much more. I nearly swallowed my tongue when her full unobscured breasts came into view. She shifted again, rubbing her thighs together.

"You are so beautiful, sweets."

I was right, the blush did extend down over the top of her breasts, and her nipples pebbled under my scrutiny. She was unable to stand still. I wasn't sure if it was because she wasn't used to standing almost naked in front of a man, or if it was because she was trying to gain some friction between her legs. If I had to guess, I'd say it was a little of both.

After another few seconds of enjoying watching her squirm, I lowered my head, deciding I had tortured both of us enough. I needed to taste her. With a long swipe of my tongue, I licked one nipple while I used my hand to plump and squeeze her other breast.

"Oh, God." She pushed further into me.

Once I'd spent a good amount of time lavishing both of her breasts with my mouth and hands, I lifted my head and watched as I lowered my hand down her belly to the top of her panties. I needed to make sure she was with me every step. Satisfied when she thrust her hips in my direction, I pushed under the material and felt her soft curls. The tip of my middle finger grazed her clit, and her body jerked, and her eyes flew open.

Damn, she was beautiful. Her hazel eyes were clouded over and unfocused.

"You still good?" I asked.

"Yeah. Please touch me."

"I want to kiss you, Rea, is that okay?"

She giggled and stared at me with hilarity dancing in her eyes. "Um, Clark, your hand is in my panties, and I'm begging you to touch me. Of course, you can kiss me."

I suppose my question would sound absurd to someone who didn't have any hang-ups about kissing. I hadn't allowed a woman to kiss my mouth in a very long time. If memory serves, my bitch of an ex-wife was the last person I'd kissed. Not that I'd tell that to Reagan. It made me sound like a douchebag. Which I was, but kissing to me was an act of intimacy. Yet another thing I'd have to analyze after Reagan was gone. Why the hell did I want to kiss her more than I wanted my next breath? I didn't tell her that either. Instead, I said, "Nolan. When my hands and mouth are on you, I am Nolan."

I didn't know why the fuck I'd said that. Telling her I wanted to kiss her was one thing, but demanding she call me by a name I hated was some-

Freedom

thing else entirely. It was fucked up – that's what it was.

"Please kiss me, Nolan."

Our mouths collided, our tongues touched, and I devoured her. There was no other word for it. I didn't kiss her. I didn't coax her tongue to meet mine. I inhaled her like she was my last breath.

When my middle finger started to make slow, hard circles on her clit, she bucked into me and dug her nails into my back. Hell yeah! I dipped my middle finger into her heat, gathering moisture, dragging it back up to her clit, and she bit my lip before kissing me harder.

"Please," she whined into my mouth. Before I could respond, she was back to kissing me.

I made sure the heel of my hand was over her clit before I pushed a finger into her pussy and groaned at the tightness. She pulsed and throbbed against my finger and ground down on the heel of my hand. There was no use trying to take a calming breath or thinking about baseball stats; she was so sexy I was going to shoot off in my boxers like a teenager. And I couldn't bring myself to care. Somehow, knowing that it was Reagan that could make me come without even touching my cock drove me insane.

"That's it, Reagan, ride my hand. You're so

83

fucking wet you're dripping." I curled my finger up and added pressure, causing her to buck and try and pull away. "Relax, baby. Let it happen, don't pull away from it."

"I can't, Nolan. I can't."

"You can. You're close. I can feel you squeezing and clenching my finger. Fuck my fingers and let go." I pulled my finger out and quickly pushed back in with two. Her hips thrust forward, and she let out a low guttural moan. "You are so goddamn beautiful. I want you to come for me."

Lowering my head, I took her nipple into my mouth and sucked hard. Reagan flew apart in my arms, detonating my orgasm. I didn't need any touching or friction, just having my fingers inside Reagan knowing that I brought her off for the first time was enough. I slowed my pace, coming to a stop when I felt the last of her orgasm slip away. I kissed up her chest and neck until I ended with a final peck on her lips.

"Wow," she whispered. I didn't know what I'd expected when I looked at her face, but a huge breathtakingly beautiful smile was not it. No signs of regret or embarrassment were present - just a look of wonderment. "Holy shit. I think I understand now what all the fuss is about. If that happens every time you orgasm, then sign me up because that is fantastic." Her excitement was contagious, and I found myself chuckling right along with her. "Seriously Nolan, how have I gone my whole life not ever having one of those. I mean at first it felt kinda weird like I got hot all over, then it almost felt like it was going to hurt, so I wanted to get away from it, but when you started pushing up top and rubbing really hard I felt like I was going to convulse. Then, holy shit, when you bit my nipple I couldn't control it, it was like a bright flash of heat took over... ohmygod I'm doing it again. I'm so sorry."

Her pretty face flushed and she face planted on my chest.

"Look at me, Rea," I urged.

"Uh-uh, no way. I want the earth to open and swallow me whole. I cannot believe I just said all that to you. It's totally embarrassing, like I'm imparting some sort of wisdom on you."

"News flash, I have a dick." I laughed.

"What does having a dick have to do with my verbal vomit?" she groaned.

"Well, seeing as I have a dick, I've never experienced the female orgasm."

"So, it's not like you haven't given them before." Her words were still muffled, and I could feel her lips against my bare chest as she spoke, causing my spent cock to start to stir again.

"Giving them and hearing what happened to your body are two entirely different things. As much as I enjoy your mouth so close to my skin, I need you to look at me please." I waited for her to look at me, then I continued. "Never be embarrassed to talk to me about anything. Especially what we do together. I want to know what feels good to you, and how it makes you feel. I love that you felt good and are excited and happy, so excited you wanted to tell me about it. Never hide who you are, it is stunning and the most precious gift you can give."

The look on Reagan's face said it all – I had lost my ever-loving mind.

"Okay."

"Change of plans. Shower before coffee. I'm a little messy and need a clean pair of boxers."

Reagan's eyes widened, and she looked down, then back up, meeting my eyes. "Is that all me? Holy crap, Nolan, I'm sorry."

I bite back a laugh, but barely. "No, baby, that is me. You were so fucking sexy when you were fucking my fingers and coming on my hand I didn't even try and stop it and joined you."

I was not only shocked I'd admitted that to her, but that I came in my pants in the first place.

"You... you know... but I didn't touch you back. How is that possible?" she stammered.

"I'm wondering the same thing," I mumbled. "Join me in the shower?"

She nodded and followed me to the bathroom. Much to my surprise she didn't try and cover herself, and when we stopped, so I could turn on the water she allowed her eyes to roam freely, only smiling at me when I caught her licking her lips again.

I was in hell – the fiery pits of the underworld – a place where I had to keep my wayward cock from finding the slick heat it desired. This was going to be the longest shower of my life.

8

I should've been self-conscious that my shirt was on the floor next to the door, where a man that I'd only known for under forty-eight-hours had taken it off and tossed it aside. Then, I essentially had sex with his hand while standing against his bedroom door after I'd busted in his room uninvited and was thrown on the floor while he was in the grips of a nightmare. I should've been horrified at my actions. I was behaving like a trollop, but I couldn't muster up the mortification. I was giddy with excitement.

There we were, standing in his bathroom waiting for the water to heat up, me half naked with only my panties on, and Clark was naked as a jaybird. Of course, he had nothing to be worried about; he was hot – all muscle and male goodness. His scars added to his badass appeal. Jesus holy moly, I'd never wished I had a photographic memory more than at this moment; not when I was cramming for finals, not in the middle of a presentation in front of advertising execs, never. But right now, I wished I had one; I wanted to memorize this moment so I'd never forget the way he looked.

"Reagan?"

Shit, was he talking to me?

"Sorry, what?"

"You ready?" he chuckled.

"Yeah."

I started to step toward the shower enclosure when he shook his head. "Take your panties off before you get in."

Crap. He must think I'm a complete dumbass. First, I blathered on about having an orgasm – which was out-of-this-world-fantastic - now I'm getting in the shower with my undies on. Geez.

He held his hand out and pulled me into the stall in front of him, taking the brunt of the spray on his back.

"Is it too hot?" he asked.

"No. The hotter, the better."

"Is that so?" I could hear the humor in his voice. "Good to know."

Thankfully he was behind me and missed the heat that had hit my cheeks, which was stupid considering I was standing in the shower with the man.

By the time we exited the shower, I was a puddle of goo. My muscles were loose and relaxed after Clark had massaged every inch of my body while he soaped me up. When I protested, he shushed me and told me he enjoyed touching me. When I asked if I could return the favor he'd refused and explained that if I put my hands on him, we'd spend the rest of the morning in his bed. Which did not sound like a problem to me, so I pushed, and he still said no. It was hard to believe that someone as inexperienced and ordinary as myself could test his control. I wouldn't have if I hadn't seen (and felt) his hard-on throughout our shower. And what a spectacular hard-on it was.

Now, I know I may not have had a lot of first-hand knowledge of dicks, but I do have the internet and have watched some videos trying (unsuccessfully) to masturbate. It was safe to say I knew a big dick when I saw one. I wouldn't call it a scary monster cock but holy hell it was close. I wanted to ask him if he got light-headed when blood rushed to the muscle to harden. I mean, it could happen, right?

I totally would've asked if I could've formed a coherent thought, but I couldn't. His hands were on me drying me off with a fluffy white towel that was unusually warm and soft.

"You have soft towels, and it's warm like it just came out of the dryer."

Dammit, I wished I had some duct tape to put over my mouth so I stopped saying the lamest shit.

"Towel warmer." He stopped rubbing the material down my leg and motioned toward the metal rack on the wall. "When I'm out on a mission there's no comfort, everything we carry with us is out of necessity. When I'm at home, I want comfort and a small amount of luxury, even if it's a towel."

"Makes sense. Do you go out on missions often?" He didn't answer, and I worried I'd unknowingly put my foot in my mouth – I did that a lot. "Never mind. That was rude of me to ask."

"No, it wasn't. You can ask me anything you want, but you have to understand there are things about my job I cannot answer. It's not because I don't want to, it's literally because I cannot. To answer your question, there is no easy answer for that. There are times when we've been gone months on end. One mission ends and something new heats up, and before we make it stateside, we are rerouted somewhere else. However, as of late, knock on wood, things have been quiet, and we've been home more than gone. But don't repeat that to the guys. If they knew I said that out loud and we get sent away they'll kick my ass." Clark stood and smiled down at me. Damn, he was tall.

"Why would they blame you?"

"We're all a little superstitious."

"Like don't walk under a ladder and all that?" I asked.

Clark led us out of the bathroom and went to his drawer, pulling out one of his tees and yanking it over my head. Alrighty then, I guess I'm wearing a t-shirt dress this morning. I fought the urge to smell his shirt, but only because Clark might find it creepy.

"Not that bad. But we all have things we do and don't do before we leave on a trip. There are things we bring with us for good luck and protection. Then there are things you don't ever say – like it's been slow or I'm bored. That is just asking for shit to hit the fan, and we get called up on an op."

"You never told me what a Combat Applications Group was."

"Umm, right. I was distracted." Clark nuzzled into my neck. "You smell so good."

"Message received loud and clear. I'll stop

asking." Besides, Clark kissing the side of my neck was way better than talking about Army stuff that I would never need to know or understand.

"Combat Applications Group is a special mission unit, also known as SFOD, Special Forces Operational Detachment, or Delta team."

"Mmm, sounds pretty badass. God, it feels good when you kiss behind my ear. My arms break out in goosebumps when you touch me there." I wish he'd forget about coffee and conversation and take us right to bed, but unfortunately, he'd already pulled on a pair of sweatpants. "It really is a shame."

"What is?" he asked, straightening and pulling us toward the door. He seemed to do that a lot. When Clark wanted me to follow him, he simply grabbed my hand and moved me where he wanted me; he didn't ask me to follow or ask if I was ready, he just tugged on my hand, and I went.

"You covering up your impressive dick."

When he tossed his head back and roared with laughter, it made all the embarrassment I felt worth it. Just like in his Jeep in front of Jasper's house, when Clark laughed, something I didn't think he did very often, my insides warmed.

"Damn woman, you don't hold back, do you? You call it as you see it." He laughed.

"Sorry." I tried to pull my hand from his grip, my awkwardness around him off the charts. Why couldn't I keep my freaking mouth shut?

"Don't be. It is a whole new experience for me. Most women like to play guessing games. It's like walking through a minefield. One thing I hate is guessing. I love that you say what is on your mind, especially when it's my cock that you're thinking about." The accompanying wink made me want to jump him and shove him on the couch. "Relax, and I'll make the coffee. How do you take yours?"

I sat on the couch and answered, "Black, please."

"Huh," Clark said and looked down at me smiling.

"What's huh mean?"

"You're full of surprises. I figured you for a cream and sugar kinda girl."

"I used to be. But through college, there were plenty of times I needed the caffeine. I learned to drink what was available. So, I guess I'm not all that picky. If it's strong enough to grow hair on your chest or make you feel like you have enough energy to run a marathon, it's perfect."

"Good to know." Clark walked into his kitchen and pulled out two K-cups from the cabinet and set up the instant one cup coffee maker with water.

Once the machine was gurgling and spitting water, he turned to me. "You don't know much about the Army, do you?" he asked.

"No, not really. I don't know anyone in the military except Jasper, and he never talked about the Army to me when he came back to visit. I don't even really know what he does, other than maybe test equipment, or something like that. I assume you do the same since you work with him. Does that bother you?"

"No. I like that you don't know anything. Most of the women around here are well versed in the Army lifestyle. They are trying their hardest to hook up with a military man. I know that sounds bad, but the majority of women I come in contact with are Barrack Bunnies."

"Ummm, I don't know what a Barrack Bunny is."

I didn't need to know the actual meaning to know I was happy I wasn't placed in that category. It sounded an awful lot like a derogatory name.

"A woman who lurks around the base waiting for any Army guy to pay attention to them. They don't care who, what rank, or rate, they just want to hook up. Then, of course, you have the guys who are down with contractual marriages and don't mind that their fake wife has been passed around more times than the gravy boat at Thanksgiving dinner."

Clark handed me a cup of coffee and sat on the couch next to me. "Seriously? That sounds... unsanitary."

"It can be. I won't lie to you, Rea, I've been with my fair share of Barrack Bunnies. I admit it makes me a dick, but they're easy. There have been times in the past when we've come home from an op, and all I wanted was a warm body to sink into and not have to think for a few hours. A woman who didn't require work, or a whole lot of talking, was what I needed. All she was after was how many chevrons I had on my uniform and what she could brag to her girls about. I didn't have to feel bad when the exchange was over because that's all it was - an exchange."

My stomach started to twist. Is that what he thought about me? Of course, it was. I was nothing more than a warm body to pass the time with. Nothing more. Nothing special. Nothing memorable. As a matter of fact, the Barrack Bunnies had more going for them than I did. They seemed to embrace who they were, and God knows, they had way more experience than I did.

"You are not one of them," Clark said, seemingly reading my mind. "Not even close. That is just a small part of what makes this different for me. It also means that we need to talk."

Sweet baby Jesus! I didn't want to talk about sex, or what had already happened between us. Which was funny because when I was a teenager, my mom used to tell me that if I was too embarrassed to talk about sex, I wasn't ready to be having it. Now here I was, sitting on the couch next to a man that was far too sexy for me, not wanting to talk about the very act I wanted to have with him. I was acting like a child.

"I want to have sex with you."

There I said it. Unfortunately, my outburst only made me sound like an idiot. Clark nearly choked on his coffee when he turned his wide shock-filled eyes toward me. "Glad to hear it, because I want to have more than just sex with you and it would really suck if you didn't feel the same way. First things first. I'm clean. We all get tested every month for work, and I haven't been with anyone since my last test."

Oh shit, we were doing this, having a mature adult conversation about our sexual history. Right. Okay. It was the responsible thing to do, but now I had to say out loud and admit I was nowhere in his league of sexual equivalence.

"I have had two lovers. One was my senior year

of high school. I lost my virginity the weekend of prom. Don't say it, cliché I know. I was almost eighteen and just wanted it over with. We had sex a few times. It wasn't good. Then he dumped me. Number two was my sophomore year of college. The sex was equally as disappointing, but Tom was a nice guy, so it made up for it. There have been a few guys since I've made out with, but that's it."

I was seriously pathetic. Not because I didn't sleep around. I was picky about what kind of laundry soap I used; I think that I should be more particular about who got to touch and see my vagina than if Tide made my clothes smell funny or not. I felt like a pitiful girl who couldn't find a date. While I told Clark the truth, there had been a few guys I'd made out with, that number was actually three. I'd dated three men in the last three years. I had kissed a total of six guys my entire life.

Maybe if I learned some good old fashioned social skills men wouldn't run for the hills as fast as their legs could carry them.

9

Two. She told me she'd only seen two men naked before, so I shouldn't have been so surprised, but I was. I also knew that I was the only man to ever bring her to orgasm; however, the thought that she'd only had two lovers did crazy shit to me.

I wanted to fuck her until she forgot there were two men before me, then lock her in my house and make sure there was never a number four, but I knew that would never happen. The attraction I had for her would die off after a few days, a week if we were lucky, then she'd be gone.

Yeah, keep telling yourself that – jackass.

What the fuck was wrong with the men in Montana? She was beautiful, smart, and had a wicked sense of humor. The girl had me laughing more than any person I'd ever met. That was what made her so irresistible; she made me laugh without thought or trying to do so. She always had me in stitches. It wouldn't be long before some lucky son-of-a-bitch snatched her up and married her.

"What else do we need to talk about?" she asked, pulling me from my stupor.

What else? My mind went blank when she fidgeted with her now empty coffee cup and set it on the table. Just enough of my shirt she was wearing pulled up, exposing the outside of her thigh when she leaned toward the table.

"It's important to me that you understand I don't want us being physical to change our friendship. I like you and don't want any hurt feelings when this ends. I can't give you more than a few nights."

"You already explained that. I told you I understood. What's the problem?" she snapped.

I brushed a few strands of her shiny golden hair away from her face and left my hand on her cheek. "No problem. Just double checking we're on the same page. I don't want to screw this up."

"We're on the same page. Orgasms. Nothing more." She leaned into my touch, making my cock stir. "Now, we've talked. Can we go back to your room?"

This girl was going to be my downfall. No ifs, ands, or buts. She was going to kill me.

"Yeah. We can." I didn't waste any more time talking; I tugged her hand, and she stood with me. She followed me into my bedroom, not bothering to close the door behind us as I led us to my bed. I was thankful that I'd never had another woman in my house or my bed. It seemed fitting that Reagan would forever be the only woman who'd grace my personal space. Long after she was gone, there was no doubt I'd lie in my bed and remember her.

"Last chance to change your mind," I told her and reached for the hem of my tee. Even in the over-sized shirt, with her hair wet from our shower, she looked stunning.

"I want you to fuck me." The blush told me she wasn't used to saying those words. As a matter of fact, I'd bet my retirement she'd never uttered them to another man. Yet here she was, bold as brass, telling me exactly what she wanted.

"I'm not going to fuck you." I placed a finger to her lips when she tried to protest. "I'm going to lie you out, spread your sexy thighs, and eat you until you come on my tongue and fingers. After that, I'm going to clean you up and take you to get some break-fast before I go to work. Tonight, after I cook you dinner and we talk some more, if you still feel the same way, I will fuck you until you see stars. But not until then. I want you spending the day thinking about what it will be like to have this..." I grabbed her hand and pressed it against my cock. Her fingers flexed, and I pushed myself harder against her now rubbing palm. "Replace my finger. Image what I can do to you with my cock if I can make you come around my finger." I pulled the tee over her head and tossed in on the floor, leaving her naked in front of me. "You are fucking beautiful Reagan. All of you, inside and out. I've never met someone so extraordinary. Get up on the bed."

She scrambled to do my bidding. I stopped her when she tried to drop to her back. "Don't move."

My hands went to her ass, and I had to force myself to go slow.

"But... you can... see my... ass," she grouched.

"Yeah babe, I can. I see everything from this angle. I've been dying to get my hands on your sweet ass since I saw you. You were listening to Sam Hunt, and my first thought was that song was written for you. A body like yours, soft in all the right places and tight and strong where it matters, needs to be worshipped. I'm having to use all my control to go slow." I squeezed the toned flesh of her ass, and she moaned. "Has anyone ever gone down on you?"

I don't know why I asked her that. I almost told her not to tell me when she pushed her ass back into my grip and answered. "Never."

I lowered my head and flattened my tongue, licking her from slit to ass, getting my first taste of her.

"So damn sweet, Reagan. Crawl onto the bed a little farther. Perfect."

With one more swipe of my tongue, I pulled away so I could lie on my back under her, essentially having her sit on my face. Using both my thumbs, I spread her wide and went to work.

It didn't take long for her to start grinding her pussy on my face. The throbbing in my cock intensified each time she rocked her hips.

"Nolan," she panted. I was too busy to answer her verbally, but my thumb added more pressure on her clit. Her legs were trembling, and I could feel her pulling at the sheets near my head. "Nolan."

"Relax, Rea."

"I can't. I'm afraid I'll lose my balance and suffocate you."

Making the decision not to argue with her about whether or not I'd let her suffocate me, I quickly pulled out from under her and flipped her on her back. My fingers found her wet heat and my mouth latched on to her clit, sucking hard. Reagan squirmed and pulled my hair.

"Oh my god."

"Now let go and come in my mouth."

I went back to work on her clit and didn't let up until I felt her tighten around my finger. When she finally let out a guttural moan, I slowed down, gently licking her, bringing her back down.

After a few beats, she opened her eyes and gazed down at me.

"Holy hell! That was awesome."

My lips twitched, and I smiled against her thigh. That was an understatement. She was stunning when she let go. My cock couldn't wait to get inside of her.

After I cleaned her up and gave her back my tee, she slipped out of my room to get dressed for the day. When she emerged from the guest room, looking stunning, I couldn't help the smugness that crept into my stride as I moved to the front door. I was almost positive I was strutting. Her cheeks were still flushed, and she had a smile on her face that screamed satisfied. There was no way that Jasper would miss the look. No man would.

The conversation at breakfast was light. She told me a little about the company she was working for in Florida and what her job in public relations entailed. She was passionate and smart; there was no limit on how much this woman impressed me.

I was relieved when I saw Jasper had already left for the base, but it reminded me I was running late.

"Thanks for breakfast," Reagan said and reached for the door.

"I'm the one that should be thanking you." I was happy when the pink in her cheeks made an appearance. "I'll be around to pick you up around five."

"Okay."

I watched her as she made her way to the front door and knocked. When Emily opened it, she turned and waved, a huge smile on her pretty face.

Yeah, there was no way Reagan knew how to play it cool and run a game on a man. Her goofy wave was proof positive.

10

"'Bout time your lazy ass showed up," Lenox called from across the room. I scanned the space, noting I was the last one to arrive.

Levi was at his computer not bothering to spare me a glance when he asked, "Dude, are you wearing cologne?"

I tossed my keys on my desk next to his and answered with a middle finger, though I doubt he noticed as he pounded away on his keyboard.

"Busy morning?" Blake added.

At that moment I regretted encouraging her to move down to Georgia to give Levi's ass a second chance. I had to pull a few strings and call in a favor with the Commander to get her assigned to the 707. Neither Blake nor Levi knew the lengths I'd gone to, to ensure her transfer went through. Blake fit in with the team seamlessly. She was a necessary and welcomed addition. Not only was she a kick-ass field agent but her instincts were spot on. She'd saved Levi's life, uncaring she could've been killed in the process. Anyone who would lay their life down for one of my brothers had my gratitude and loyalty. However, right now, I wanted to gag her ass before she could further encourage the guys to bust my balls.

I ignored her and studied the blueprints and HVAC schematic on the big screen mounted on the wall.

"What rig is that?" I asked Jasper as he considered the monitor as well.

"The Horizon III," he answered and scowled at me. "How's Reagan?"

"Fine." His eyes narrowed at my short answer. The trouble with working with a team where you literally bled together, killed together, and saved each other's lives, it was nearly impossible to keep secrets. We knew each other too well. "I dropped her off at your house before I came in."

"Good. Em wanted her input on the new wedding plans."

"How are those coming?" I asked.

"Same as last night when we talked about them. What aren't you telling me?"

"Nothing."

Everything.

What was I going to tell him? Oh, well, I finger fucked her to her first orgasm, then I showered with her, after that I ate her out until she exploded on my tongue and it was so fucking sweet I can still taste her. But don't worry, I fed her breakfast. And tonight, I plan on fucking her senseless because she makes me lose my ever-loving mind. Yeah, I liked my balls too much to tell him all of that.

"Can we get back to work? I swear it's turned into a daytime drama around here," Levi said as if he didn't start this line of commentary with his cologne comment.

"Where is that rig located?" I asked, thankful for the change of topic.

"In The Gulf. One hundred and thirty miles off the coast of Texas. The more important question is why are there tugs still operating out to an abandoned platform," Blake answered.

"Do you have satellite of the rig?" I asked.

"No, not yet. We only now have enough intel to request a drone feed. The actual deep-water well was capped five years ago, but the platform has remained in position," she added.

"Can it move?" Lenox asked.

"Yes. It is a semi-submersible and is moored to the seafloor. Alger Energy has left a fifty-million-dollar floating city sitting in The Gulf," Blake answered. "I started watching the patterns of the oil rig tug boats leaving out of southern Texas when there was chatter from eco-terrorists about planting explosives on the platforms. The chatter came from a group based out of Brownsville. When a tug started making trips from South Padre Island out to the Horizon III, I concentrated on those trips to and from."

"I don't get it. Why did that boat gain your attention?" Levi inquired.

"First, because it was close to Brownsville and second, South Padre is not a usual port for an employee transport boat to leave from. Also, a transport boat takes workers to the rig, drops them off, picks up the crew that is rotating off and comes back to shore the same day. This boat goes out and stays out anywhere from five to ten days, sometimes longer. There is no rhyme or reason to how long it stays. One time I went down there and waited for the boat to return and no crew came off. I also ran the images I took of the captain through facial recognition and got no hits. I sent the image to your tablets and to the Commander."

Before I could get my tablet out of my desk, Levi had the image on the screen. White male, early thirties. A little young to be a tugboat captain, but not unheard of. His features look to be American or European descent. There was nothing unique about him. Even his clothes were nondescript. No name tags, brand names, or logos visible. He looked like any other fisherman from the area.

"All of the images I have of him are the same. Mr. John Doe is plain and smart. I followed him into a local bar, and he went to the back where the restrooms were and never returned, leaving his beer and lunch untouched."

"Did he make you?" Levi asked, even though we all knew the answer to that.

"Not a chance," Blake smirked.

"What does the Commander say?" Lenox asked.

"We're in a wait and see holding pattern. He's approved the drone; unfortunately, this doesn't take priority, and we are about fifth in line before we get to use one. While threats to blow up an oil rig is illegal, the higher-ups don't think it's a matter of national security."

"What does your gut tell you, Blake?" I asked.

Blake's heels clicked on the floor as she paced the worn concrete floor of the hangar. I was getting ready to comment on the absurdity of her wearing business attire to the old Army outbuilding when she spoke. "Something doesn't feel right. If the group was planning on planting bombs on different rigs, why does the boat only visit an abandoned platform? Wouldn't it be traveling to multiple rigs - learning their crew rotations?" She posed it as a question, but we all understood it was her way of talking it out. "But the boat goes out at night not returning for days. It also departs from a private dock. A crew boat wouldn't do that."

"So, what are you thinking?" Lenox asked, looking closely at the blueprints of the Horizon III.

"I'm not sure. But I'd bet the chatter was code, fake. It's dumb luck we've stumbled onto something else entirely. Once we have visual on the platform, I'll have a better idea what we're dealing with."

"Shit, this thing is huge," Lenox noted.

"Almost two football fields. I told you it was a floating city."

"Why don't we go out there for a RECON op?" Jasper asked, and the rest of us simultaneously groaned. "Not that I want to go out, but fuck, I also don't want to wait weeks to find out what the hell is going on out there. I agree with Blake; something is not right."

"I mentioned that to the Commander, and he said no."

Thank fuck. I didn't want to have to leave on a mission that would take me away from Reagan when she'd only be here another few days or a few weeks tops, especially when we were just getting to the fun stuff.

"Anything else for today?" I asked.

"No."

"Not from me."

"Nope."

"No, but if you're going to PT I'll come with you," Jasper said.

Damn. That was another problem; the guys knew my daily routine. I always PT'd after our morning brief if there was nothing else pressing to take care of. Again, I couldn't lie to him without him knowing, so I was fucked. I wanted time alone to sort my head out before I went back to his house and picked up Reagan. I also needed to think about if I was going to tell him about my nightmare. If Reagan told Emily, and Emily told Jasper, and I hadn't told him myself, he'd be pissed. Rightfully so.

I hadn't had a chance to think about the best way to broach the subject without him asking a hundred questions.

"Yeah, I'm headed there now."

The drive to the base gym was quiet. I was lost in thought about Reagan when Jasper sighed and turned the stereo off. "What happened?"

"Come again?"

What the hell, could he read my mind now? He was like Professor Xavier from the X-Men the way he stared at me like he was in my head. It was unfortunate I'd left my metal helmet at home today; I needed to find another way to block his nosey ass mental exploration.

"Something happened with Reagan. Before you deny it, I'll remind you that I know every one of your tells. You look guilty as shit right now, yet surprisingly relaxed and happy. It's the happy part that is worrying me the most right now."

"You're worried because I look happy?" I chuckled.

"See, right fucking there, you laughed. What the hell is going on?"

"You have an issue with my sunny disposition?"

"Now you're... I don't know what you're doing. Joking?"

"Should I flip you off and tell you to mind your own fucking business?" I asked.

"Yes. That would be more in line with your normal temperament."

I parked and cut the ignition but made no move to exit the Jeep. We needed to talk, and there was no time like the present.

"I had a nightmare this morning." There was a lot to explain, best I start at the beginning.

"Fuck."

Jasper had been around me long enough to understand what my nightmare entailed.

"Did she hear?"

"Worse. She came into my room and tried to wake me up." I paused for a moment. "She touched me."

"Goddammit. Did you hurt her? Was she freaked out?"

"I didn't hurt her; however, we did end up on the floor. She tried to deny it, but I know she was scared."

"The dog is gone. She can come back and stay with me."

"That's not happening." There was zero chance I was letting Reagan out of my sight.

Jasper arched his eyebrow and squinted at my forceful response. "Come again?"

"She's staying with me. We talked about my nightmare, and I will make sure she understands that she's not to touch me if it happens again."

"You talked with Reagan about your nightmare?"

"Yep."

"You're gonna need to explain that to me."

This was the part I didn't want to talk to him about, the whys and wherefores of my out-of-character actions. I'd only told my team about my nightmares out of necessity. However, I didn't make a habit of telling anyone else. My team knew the bare minimum, most of which they figured out from me calling out in my sleep.

"You told her about Moses?" he asked when I didn't answer right away.

"Yes," I admitted.

The low whistle that came from Jasper spoke volumes. "Well, damn. Now you wanna explain why you're smiling?"

"Drop it."

"Not a chance," he pushed. What Jasper called my normal temperament was about to rear its ugly head. I didn't like talking about my personal life, and it'd been a long time since I had to explain myself to anyone. "Did you fuck her?"

"Careful," I warned. I didn't like hearing Jasper ask that about Rea. His flippant question made her sound like a cheap tag chaser, and that pissed me the fuck off.

"Careful? What the fuck, Clark. I saw the way the two of you were dancing around each other. She looks at you like rainbows are shooting outta your ass. And I don't think I've ever seen a woman hold your attention, let alone make you smile. I'd be pleased as fuck if I didn't know you so well."

"Care to explain what that means?"

"It means I know you. You've made it painfully clear over the years that you don't want any entanglements. You're emotionally unavailable and go to great lengths to hold yourself as far away from anything that looks like a relationship. I've watched you go home with women, and it is as sterile as you can make it. Hell, I've never seen you flirt with a woman. You wait until you're approached and propositioned, then you take her back to her place to do your business and leave. You trust no one except the team. That works for you. I get it, I really do. But there is no way Reagan will. She's young and blinded by sunshine. She doesn't have the tools to handle you."

Jasper had pretty much summed up exactly who I was and how I conducted my personal life. He was right on all accounts but one. Reagan might've been young, but she understood what this was. She wanted nothing from me. She said it herself. She was moving to Florida to start her new life.

"I didn't fuck her. I won't lie to you; things did happen. But you gotta know we did talk before anything started, and she is clear on what this is."

"And what exactly is *this*?"

Now I was pissed.

"You want details?" I asked. "Because I gotta tell you I don't think you want them any more than I want to give them to you. Before I get pissed, you have to ask yourself if I would fuck her over. And not because she's your family, but because she's Reagan. While you're asking yourself that, you can include if you trust me."

"There is not enough ear bleach in the world to make me want details." Jasper sighed and settled further into the seat. "Shit, brother. Of course, I trust you. I just wish..."

He trailed off, and I didn't wait for him to

continue his sentence before I spoke. "Then let me worry about Rea. I promise you I will handle her with care. I would rather cut off my trigger finger than hurt her. She means something to me. You're right. I don't let women close to me, and I tried to keep her at arm's length, but damn, brother, it's impossible not to fall at her feet when she acts goofy and spouts off the most ridiculous shit. She has no sense of personal space or boundaries. When she has something to say, she blurts it; social niceties be damned."

I knew I'd said too much when Jasper did nothing but stare at me. Damn, the woman had me talking too much.

"Never mind."

"Never mind, what?" I asked.

"Forget I said anything. And for the record, if you lost your trigger finger, you'd have nine other digits to use. No doubt you'd be just as proficient."

"I was gonna say, I'd rather cut off my cock, but given the conversation we're having I didn't think you'd want to hear about cock."

"You thought right."

"Great, now that we've been pussified and had a heart-to-heart, you wanna go work out? Or do you have a vaginal itch you'd like to discuss?"

Jasper roared with laughter and wiped his eye.

"Christ. Happiness looks good on you. I think I can get used to this new sunny disposition. Trust me when I tell you it is more than a step up. You're much more tolerable this way."

He opened the door, jumped out, and shut the door. I heard the slam of the metal but didn't move.

Happiness?

Is this what happiness felt like?

11

It was nearing four o'clock when Jasper walked into the house. Emily and I had spent the day going over wedding plans and trying to find a new venue. Thankfully she'd narrowed them down to two; it cut down on the time we needed to go across town and look at them. I wanted to be back to her house by five, so I wouldn't be late when Clark got there.

I had been floating on cloud nine all day, but as the hours passed, I was becoming more and more anxious to see Clark. Not because I was nervous or I'd changed my mind about where I want our friendship to go. I found myself missing him. There had been several times throughout the day I'd wanted to text him and tell him something funny, but I refrained. He'd given me his number *in case I needed anything*. I didn't think that included random text messages about songs I'd heard on the radio or funny memes I'd found.

Spending time with Emily was just what I needed. It hadn't even been ten minutes after Clark had dropped me off when she brought up Liz. At first, I was a little uncomfortable, but she quickly eased any awkwardness when she told me how Jasper had come home from Montana and told her all about his trip. She'd even read Liz's journal to Jasper. It made me happy that my sister was talked about, that Jasper hadn't hidden her away. She didn't deserve to be a secret; my sister was too good for that. Emily asked a lot of questions about her, general ones about who Liz was as a person. She listened while I told her funny stories about the three of us growing up and wanted to know more about Jasper as a teenager. I would've thought it was weird talking about Liz to Emily, but it wasn't. Em wasn't jealous or resentful of Liz at all. At the end of our talk, Emily had cried, telling me how sorry she was and how much she loved Liz and Alesha too.

When we finished our talk about my sister, we dove into wedding plans. I was grateful she hadn't asked me about Clark. I didn't think he'd want me talking to anyone about what happened, even though I wanted to pull Emily on the couch and tell her all about my first orgasm and my second. I felt like a teenager with a secret crush on the cute boy in school. I guess in a way I was. Only tonight I got to have sex with him too. I was being ridiculous, and I knew it. Only I couldn't stop myself; actually I didn't want to. I was excited and happy. It was nice to be those things for a change.

"Hey, Mr. Walker, how was your day?" I asked in a singsong voice when Jasper came into view.

"Well, aren't you chipper today?" he answered.

I smiled wide at my friend and prayed that I wasn't turning red.

"I'm always chipper."

Jasper's smile was too knowing when he looked down at me to where I sat on the couch. "If you say so, Rea. Clark wanted me to tell you he'd be here in thirty minutes. He needed to stop by the store."

"Okay. You trying to rush me out the door before Jason gets back from his afternoon with his grandma?" I winked at him and wiggled my eyebrows.

"I don't know; you're the one that looks pretty excited to get out of here and get back to Clark's," he returned.

Whelp. I didn't have a comeback to that, so I changed the subject. "Looks like we got your wedding back on track, and Em only had to postpone it for a month."

"Yeah, Em texted me the info and pictures of the new B&B. It looks great. Honestly, I'd be happy marrying her in the backyard, but I know that's not what she wants. I don't mind either way as long as at the end of the day, her and Jason are mine."

"I love that."

I totally loved that Jasper had found someone that made him so happy. After losing Liz and Alesha the way he did, I wanted him to be happy. I was saddened when Emily told me that when she first met Jasper, she thought he didn't like kids and he bailed as soon as he found out she had a child. I knew it took a lot for Jasper to face his fears and seek me out after all these years. I guess in my grief I hadn't considered all the guilt he was carrying around. I should've known. And now I felt like an asshole for not being the one to reach out to Jasper years ago. I knew that Liz hadn't been upset with him and she never would've wanted him to hurt. Instead, I selfishly kept my sister's thoughts and her journal all to myself, not wanting to give up even the smallest part of my sister away, even if that part of her didn't belong to me.

"We need to talk." The grimace Jasper wore told me I wasn't going to like what he wanted to discuss.

"Okay." I drew the word out and settled back on the couch.

"Clark."

One word that held so much meaning but told me nothing.

"What about him?"

"He...um... told me." Jasper cleared his throat and looked so uncomfortable I would've laughed at his discomfort if I didn't think I was going to throw up. What had Clark told him? Had he changed his mind already and sent Jasper to let me down?

"Told you what?" I asked.

Jasper's brows drew together, and he fidgeted with his phone, spinning it in his hands.

"Spit it out, Jasper. Geez. You're freaking me out."

"Sorry. He told me he had a nightmare and you shook him awake."

"I did. I apologized to him. Is he still upset with me?"

Damn. I thought that we'd moved past me barging in his room. At least I thought we had after he gave me a few mind-numbing orgasms. He'd also made it clear that I had an open invitation to his bedroom.

"No, he's not upset with you. I just wanted to make sure that you're okay and he didn't hurt you. He said that you were scared even though you played it off that you weren't."

"Of course, I was scared. I heard him yelling for someone to kill him. When I opened his door, he was fighting and twisting in his sleep." I left the part out about Clark crying. That was no one's business, not even Jasper's. "I couldn't take it seeing him so tortured. I didn't know I shouldn't touch him, so I tried to shake him awake. That's all."

"That's not all. He said that he threw you to the ground and when he woke up he was on top of you pinning you to the floor."

Well, he did do that, but I didn't want to tell Jasper that once Clark had woken up my fear quickly morphed into something else and I wanted nothing more than to kiss the lingering agony away.

"It was nothing really. Hell, you've pinned me harder when we were kids, and you tried to tickle me until I peed my pants. Something I'll never forgive you for, by the way. There's nothing funny about a thirteen-year-old peeing her pants."

"Dammit Rea, this is serious."

"Fine. Yes, when I touched him he grabbed me, and we fell to the floor. I hit my head on the nightstand and then the floor. For a few seconds, I was scared shitless. It hurt, but it was nothing compared to seeing Clark in pain. When he looked at me, his eyes were dead, and he was lost in a faraway place. I couldn't watch him like that. I had to stop it."

There was a noise behind me that sounded like a cross between and growl and grumble. Either way, it wasn't a happy sound. I closed my eyes and prayed Clark hadn't slipped in the house unnoticed. When I refocused on Jasper, he was looking over my shoulder. His lips pursed together so tight they were flat. But his eyes weren't angry; they were full of sympathy.

"Why didn't you tell me you hit your head?"

Yep. Clark was behind me.

"I was fine."

"That's not what I asked you." His voice sent shivers through my body. "You should've told me I hurt you when I asked."

"*You* didn't hurt me. That's why I didn't tell you. I didn't want you to blame yourself or be upset. Besides, it was no big deal. It smarted for a minute, that's all. By the time we got off the floor, I wasn't even thinking about my head."

Not that I wanted to admit why I wasn't thinking about my hurt head anymore. Sweet Jesus, I could still picture the outline of his dick through his boxers. My cheeks heated at the memory. Damn, I wanted to hurry and get back to Clark's. Jasper cleared his throat, bringing my attention back to him. His arched eyebrow made me want to cover my face in embarrassment.

"Why was that, Rea?" He was teasing me, trying to break the tension. While I appreciated the effort, there was no way I was telling Jasper why.

"I could tell you, but I'm sure you'd need electroshock therapy to wipe the images from your memory." I winked and smiled, hoping that Jasper would understand I was only half kidding with him.

"This isn't funny. I hurt her. And the two of you are cracking jokes. The fuck?" Clark grouched.

"Geez, Mr. Grumpy. I'm fine. I tapped my head I didn't get a concussion."

"Reagan."

"Nolan."

Jasper roared with laughter, holding his stomach as he fell back against the chair he'd sat in.

I stood and faced Clark for the first time since he'd snuck into the room.

I tried to ignore Jasper's hilarity and said, "I

know it's not a joke. There is nothing funny about you being in the grips of horrible memories. But I wasn't hurt. I promise. I was frightened, yes. However, I knew you wouldn't actually hurt me. I know now not to touch you. Next time I'll stand across the room and throw something at you so you can't reach me."

"I'm dangerous, Rea."

"You said that before, and I don't believe you. The second you heard me crying you loosened your grip and woke up. If you were dangerous and were going to hurt me, you could've. But you didn't."

"Fuck," Clark muttered.

Time to move on. "What'd you get at the store? I'm starving, and you had nothing at your house to eat."

"There's plenty of food in the fridge."

"Umm... it's full of veggies, healthy crap, and yogurt. My body is not a temple, and I require salt, grease, and something fried almost daily." Clark's lips twitched just as I'd hoped. "While I fully appreciate that you take physical fitness and healthy eating seriously, my body may go into shock without its outrageously horrible dietary regimen."

"I grabbed you some soda and a few bags of chips."

"Thank you. Thank you. Thank you. I thought I was going to have to choke down carrots as a midnight snack."

"I can think of better things other than carrots," Clark muttered under his breath.

"If you finish that sentence, after I'm done puking I'll throat punch your ass." Jasper made a gagging sound.

"Geez Jasper, get your mind outta the gutter. I'm sure Clark was simply going to remind me that he had celery in the crisper as well. Fewer calories."

"No, I wasn't." Clark laughed.

"On that note, I'm going to find my woman. Both of you out."

It was my turn to gag. As happy as I was for Jasper and Emily, the last thing I wanted to picture was Jasper and anything remotely close to sex.

"Gross. I'm leaving."

I grabbed my purse and headed for the door.

"Hey." I turned back to look at Jasper. "Thanks for helping Em with the wedding."

"My pleasure. You found a good one." I smiled at him.

"I know I did."

He returned the smile, but it didn't reach his

eyes. I didn't want him to ever be uncomfortable about telling me how much he loved Emily.

"I wish Liz were here to meet her, you know she would've loved her. She's perfect for you in every way. But you would've been screwed when they ganged up on you." I laughed, remembering all the practical jokes Liz and I pulled on Jasper. "With the three of us around, you'd never be safe."

That pulled a real smile from Jasper. "Shit. I think I can still smell the burning hair from the time you thought it would be funny to put hair removal shit in my body wash."

"Wait, dude, you use body wash?" Clark chuckled.

"That's what Liz and I thought. Jasper had showered at our house after he went hunting with our dad. We found his body wash and Liz may have added a little Nair hair removal to the bottle. It was too easy."

It was hilarious is what it was. The next day Jasper had missing patches of hair on his legs. Lucky for him it had been Fall, and he could wear jeans to hide his bald spots.

"What if I would've washed my hair with it?" Jasper grumped.

"Well then, you would've been bald," I laughed.

"Whatever. I'm going to go find my woman."

"She's out back in the gym doing yoga," I told him.

"Fucking brilliant." Jasper wagged his eyebrows like a total creeper.

"Yep, we're leaving. See you tomorrow."

12

The drive back to my house had been... relaxing. I listened to Reagan tell me about her day out with Emily looking at new venues for the wedding. She was animated when she spoke, bringing the story alive not just with words but her hands as well. Reagan hadn't sat still the entire drive. I tried to think if I'd ever enjoyed listening to a woman speak more but couldn't think of a time. I was happy she felt more at ease around Emily now. I wanted to ask her why that was but didn't want to draw attention to it, so I let it go.

Now I was sitting on my back deck with a belly full of food and a beer in my hand. Reagan was sitting in a chair next to me with her feet pulled up on the edge and her chin resting on her knees, looking at me patiently to answer a question I hadn't realized she'd asked. I was too busy contemplating the softness of her skin when I'd licked up her thighs earlier this morning. Her skin was smooth and felt fantastic on my tongue. I wanted more of that, more of her. My cock had been throbbing in my pants from the moment I'd walked into Jasper's house, and her beauty had struck me. It had only deflated for a moment when I was reminded I'd thrown her to the floor during my nightmare.

"I'm sorry, what'd you ask?"

"How was your day?" she asked again.

"It was fine. Normal day at the office."

"I forgot to tell you earlier; you look hot in your uniform."

"Thanks," I chuckled, still taken aback by her candor.

"Why did you tell Jasper about what happened?" She turned fully to face me.

I thought about how to explain why I'd told Jasper.

"For a few reasons. The most important being I don't want to lie to him."

"Not telling him isn't a lie," she said.

"It is if I'm not telling him because I want to keep it a secret. Which I don't. He'd be pissed if he'd heard it from you or Emily before I'd told him. I could've seriously hurt you. I knew I'd shocked the guys when I suggested you stay with me. I saw the worried look on Jasper's face. He cares about and feels responsible for you. I had to tell him."

"Why would they be shocked - because you were being nice? Emily had said something about none of you guys being nice. Honestly, I didn't understand what she meant by that. I still don't. You all seem nice to me."

"They were shocked because I don't invite people to my house, and especially not to spend the night. The guys have all been here, but I don't like outsiders in my space. He also knows that I still dream about Moses. It doesn't happen often, but it does happen." I thought about what Emily had told her about none of us being nice and wondered what had prompted that comment. "I can't tell you why Emily said that unless you give me some context."

"We were leaving to go get the pizza, and she had the wrong idea about the two of us. I told her that you were just being nice to me. That's when she said that you weren't nice."

Not for the first time today, or the day before, I thought about how fucked I was. Reagan's frankness was something I only knew from my team. Women played games; they acted coy and cute. There was always some ulterior motive behind their actions. Reagan didn't realize that she'd told me that she and Em had been talking about me, or that she'd been trying to make excuses for my attention. She hadn't told Emily that *she* wasn't interested, she said that *I* wasn't.

"Emily was right. I'm not nice in that way. I wouldn't have wanted you to go get pizza with me if I wasn't enjoying your company and wanted to spend more time with you, even though I knew I should've been keeping my distance."

"Why should you stay away from me?" Reagan's forehead wrinkled, and she started to bite her bottom lip, something I noticed she did when she was nervous or embarrassed. I immediately remembered her worrying her lip when we were in my room when I had her pressed against my door, and my cock jerked thinking about her being nervous around me. I liked that she didn't have much experience. In the short time we'd be together, I could teach her all the pleasure of lovemaking.

What. The. Fuck? Not lovemaking. Fucking. Sex. Shagging. That's what we'd have. There would be no love involved.

I tipped my beer back and took the last swig

before I answered, deciding she should have the same honesty she'd given me.

"Because I wanted you more than I should for a variety of reasons. The first being that I can't offer you anything but a few weeks. Another was that I'm ten years older than you. Then there was the fact that my attraction to you is more than physical. Your honesty and lack of head games is just as much of a turn on as your beauty."

"Past tense."

I studied her for a moment, not understanding her statement. "What is past tense?"

"Your reasons. You said, *was*, those excuses are in the past, correct? I mean, you haven't changed your mind."

Christ this girl had no issue calling me to the carpet. "No, Rea, I haven't changed my mind. And I'm assuming by your question you haven't either."

"I spent the whole day thinking about tonight. I couldn't wait until five when I knew you'd be back to Jasper's to pick me up. And not because I wanted to fall into bed with you – though I totally do and thought a lot about what it would be like, but I found that I missed being around you."

The lump in my throat was hard to swallow. I should've done the smart, honorable thing, and gently explained to Reagan that we couldn't progress any further. Her admission about missing me was exactly what I was worried about. Emotions and feelings had to be kept out of any sex we were going to have.

Only I didn't; I couldn't, because I'd missed the hell out of her all day, too. She was all I'd thought about. I'd pulled my phone out several times over the hours to text her and ask her what she was doing for no other reason than I wanted to know. Spending time with her was not a good idea. Sinking into her warm body was going to be a life-changing mistake – one I couldn't stop myself from making.

I had no idea how Reagan had come to mean something to me in such a short amount of time, just that she had. I couldn't have said I was in love with her, but it was clear that I could be. That was all the reason I should've needed to put a stop to us. But, again, I wouldn't. I needed her too badly.

"You ready to go in? It's getting a little chilly."

"I am if you are," she said and stood when I did.

When we were in the house she almost made me drop my empty beer bottle when she blurted out, "Just so I know, after we're done tonight, are you going to tell me to go back to my room?"

"Come again?" Was she asking me if after I fucked her I was going to kick her out of my bed?

"I only want to understand. I've never done this." She motioned between the two of us.

Holy hell she was asking what I'd thought she was.

"Done what, Rea?"

"I don't know what to call it." Her pretty face started to flush, and I couldn't help the step I took toward her, placing my bottle on the counter as I moved.

"Try. Explain it to me."

"This. Us. I've never been in a man's bed only to have sex. I don't want to make any assumptions. What is proper one-night-stand protocol? When we're done am I supposed to get up and go back into the other room."

"You're not a one-night-stand," I told her and pulled her closer to me. "This is new to me, too," I admitted. "We'll do what comes naturally. No rules, no preconceived ideas."

I took her mouth in a bruising kissing, halting any further conversation. It took only seconds for her to melt into the kiss. When I felt her body fully relax, I picked her up, flexing my hands under her ass when her legs wrapped around my waist. I didn't need to break the kiss as I moved us through the living room, down the hall, and into my bedroom.

I set her on her feet and steadied her before I pulled back, disengaging our lips so I could pull her shirt over her head. As soon as the fabric cleared, I was back tasting the skin at her neck, down to the top of one breast over the other. Without pause, I unsnapped her bra and unfastened her jeans, tugging her panties and the denim down her thighs. I felt her shifting her hips toward me at the same time she stepped out of the tangled mess at her feet.

"May I?" she whispered.

I nodded against her soft belly and continued to kiss around her bellybutton. At my acquiescence, her hands were on my shoulders, moving down my back to the hem of my tee. She brought the fabric up and it gathered around my neck, forcing me to stand so she could finish removing the garment.

"You have the perfect chest," she said.

Not the sexiest thing I've ever heard, yet her declaration, accompanied with her tiny hands now on my bare skin, cause goosebumps to raise where she'd touched me.

"Pleased you think so."

I pushed the sweatpants down my legs and carefully watched Reagan for any signs that she wanted me to slow down. When I saw the flare in her eyes, I knew she was where I needed her to be. I was unable to keep my head upright as her hands traveled down my chest, over my abs, and lower still. Looking at the ceiling, I sucked in a breath and held it when she finally palmed my cock, slowly stroking up and down. Her thumb swiped the pre-come now freely leaking and smeared it around the tip before she went back to stroking me.

I stood in front of her, my hands on her hips, unable to move. My brain had disengaged, all I could do was feel. I wanted to taste her, touch her, but she held me captive with only her hand. Her movements became harder, faster, more confident. She'd added a twist to her wrist each time she pulled up to the head. I was going to lose what was left of my control if I didn't stop her.

"Enough."

"Why?" she asked and didn't still the motion.

"Because I'm going to come in your hand."

"I want you to." She gripped me tighter.

"No. The last twelve hours have been the longest of my life. All I've thought about is what it's going to be like to finally get inside of you. If I come now, we'll have to wait until I get hard again. And while I have great recovery time, even five minutes is too long."

She slowed her hand and looked up from where she'd been watching her hand and locked eyes with me.

"I agree. Five minutes is too long." Her hand fell away and without me having to ask, she crawled onto the bed, rolling until she was in the middle. Her blonde hair fanned out around her head, contrasting with the deep blue of the comforter. She looked like a fucking goddess that needed to be worshipped. By the time I was done paying homage to every part of her body, she'd feel me for days.

"Nolan?"

"Yeah?"

"Hurry."

"There is no rush. We have all night." I climbed onto the bed, my hands finding her ankles, and I pushed her legs farther apart, giving me room to move where I really wanted. Her skin pebbled as I felt my way up her calves, over her knees, to the soft skin I'd been thinking about all day. Reagan's thighs trembled under my fingertips. I knew she needed more than the featherlight touches I was giving her, but I didn't want a moment of our first time together rushed.

"I'm going to die," she whined.

After her declaration I didn't make her wait, and without warning, I lowered my head and lapped up her wetness. Her taste exploded on my tongue, and my ears took in her moans, low and guttural. Christ, I loved that sound.

It didn't take but minutes to take her to the edge with my fingers and tongue, but I pulled away when I felt her orgasm approaching.

"You're killing me."

"Hold on, sweetheart." I grabbed the condom, ripped it open, and winced when I rolled it down my cock. The latex had never felt so tight, which was a testament to how hard I was.

Carefully fisting myself, I lined up and pushed the head past the tightness that threatened to keep me out.

"Relax for me," I told her and kissed her forehead.

"Okay."

Even though she'd agreed, her body was still restrained and full of tension.

"You are so damn beautiful, sweetheart."

I kissed her cheek.

"So sexy."

I gave her a soft peck on her lips and hitched her

leg higher over my hip, and my lips went to her neck. She was wet enough that I could've pushed inside her, but the last thing I wanted was to hurt her. If I took her how I wanted to now, before she was soft and relaxed, it would be painful.

"I'm gonna make you feel so good." I continued to suck and bite on her neck and her leg around my back flexed, raising her hips. "I'm barely an inch inside of you, and I'm ready to lose my mind you feel so good." The more I talked, the more her body softened under mine. Her hips bucked up, and I pushed a little farther in. My eyes rolled as pleasure shot through my body like an electric shock.

"Please," she breathed, and I let myself go, sliding fully inside, her heat searing through the thin latex barrier.

"Holy shit," I panted. "You feel so damn good."

Without thought I pulled back and slowly pushed back in; she'd reduced my thinking to only my most primal need - to take her, to consume her, to own every part of her. I kept my strokes unhurried and methodical, with only the care to bring her pleasure. Long before I wanted it to be over, her whimpers became louder and impatient. She was tilting her hips and tightening her legs around my waist, meeting my thrusts.

"Nolan."

"I got you, baby. Let go; I'll catch you."

"Promise?" she cried.

"Promise, pretty girl, let it happen."

She convulsed and tightened around my cock, and I lost what was left of my self-control and let go with her.

"Nolan," she moaned, her short-cropped nails branding my back as they scored my skin.

Her cries of ecstasy filled the room and forever etched on my soul. There had never been, nor would there ever be, a moment that felt so right, so perfect, so fucking enduring that I couldn't stop when my heart came alive.

"Right here, baby."

13

Holy shit, I had sex with Nolan Clark. Hot, sweaty, awesome sex. I clamped my mouth shut and prayed to all things holy I didn't do something stupid like belt out hallelujah. Because that's what I wanted to do. My body was liquid, my insides were warm and placid, yet my brain was traveling a mile a minute. I wanted to dance a jig, maybe break dance, do the moonwalk, something to mark this momentous occasion. Thank God Clark's large body was still covering mine, preventing me from making a fool out of myself.

His lips found their way to my neck, and he gently kissed the sensitive skin under my jaw up to my ear. I never in a million years would've guessed that this big strong man could be so tender. He'd taken his time when he noticed I'd tensed. I didn't mean to, I wanted him so badly, but self-doubt crept in, and all the what-ifs started rolling through my head, and I couldn't turn them off. He slowed and waited me out, using his words and mouth to bring me back to the present.

When he finally let go and took me the way he wanted to, there was nothing I could do but hold on. I knew this was only sex and nothing more, but when his gaze latched onto mine while he was moving inside of me - try as I might, some of the armor I'd locked around my heart cracked. He'd warned me that all we'd ever have was a few nights, friends with benefits, extended one-night-stand, whatever you wanted to call it. I had no one to blame, but myself and I knew I'd read too much into it, but I could've sworn I saw something other than lust in his eyes.

"You okay?" he asked after he'd thoroughly obliterated any sense of self-preservation I had left.

"Okay is not a word I'd use to describe my current state of being," I told him.

"No? What word would you use?" He was teasing me, but I didn't mind.

"Do I only get one?"

"No, I guess not."

"Phenomenal. Outstanding. Awesome. Out-of-body," I answered.

"You're a nut." He laughed, just as I hoped he would. I was finding that I'd do just about anything to make the man smile. "What am I going to do with you?"

"More of that!" I offered.

"Fuck yeah, we're doing more of that. Let me get rid of this condom. Don't move."

As if I could.

He kissed my forehead and rolled out of bed. Upon his return, he got to work giving us the good stuff.

By the time we were done with round two, I no longer felt like I wanted to jump up and dance around the room. My muscles were screaming at me not to move. Clark had shifted us, placing me on top and demanded I ride him. I'd never before had the pleasure of being on top. Holy shit – the view. The sight alone was almost enough to get me off. His pecs and abs flexing and tightening was a sight to behold. When I thought I couldn't take another orgasm, Clark proved me wrong. His fingers had dug into my hips as he rocked me back and forth. I saw stars when he fastened his lips around my nipple, and I flew apart.

He cleaned us up a second time and surprised the hell out of me when he tucked me close to his side and pulled my arm over his stomach.

I was mellow and starting to drift to sleep when Clark's phone rang. He muttered a curse and plucked it off the nightstand.

"Everything okay?" he answered. There was a short pause before he said, "yeah, she's right here."

Clark rolled again so we were both sitting up, giving me a chance to look at the clock – ten p.m. not as late as I thought it was. After all our bed gymnastics it felt much later.

"Jasper," Clark said and held the phone out to me.

"Hello?"

"Hey. Sorry to bother you so late. I tried your phone, but you didn't pick up," Jasper said.

I was thankful this conversation was taking place over the phone and Jasper couldn't see what I was sure was a nice rosy blush. "Sorry about that. I think I left my phone in the living room. Umm. So. Anyway. What's up?"

Damn. I was stuttering.

"No need to explain," Jasper chuckled. Why did I just feel like I'd been caught making out on the couch by my dad? "After you left the Riverfront called. You know the place that Emily picked."

"Yeah. The new wedding venue."

"Right. Well, they called to tell her there was a mistake and the date they said they had available, they don't. Em has been upset for hours. I finally got her up to bed but not before she muttered something about this being the universes way of telling us we shouldn't get married."

"What? That's crazy."

Poor Emily had to be so upset. She loved the Riverfront.

"That's what I told her. Is there any way you can come over here tomorrow and talk to her? I'd really appreciate the help."

"Of course. I'll be there. We'll find you guys another place. Don't worry Jasper. I got your back."

"I know you do. You always did. See you tomorrow?"

"With bells," I told him, and he laughed at my silly comment.

"Night."

"Night."

"What happened?" Clark asked, but before I could answer his phone rang again.

I swiped the screen thinking Jasper had forgotten

to tell me something. Boy was I wrong. I placed the phone up to my ear, and my world imploded.

"What'd you forget?" I laughed.

"Excuse me," a woman said.

"Oh. I'm sorry. I thought you were someone else."

I looked at Clark and didn't know what I was supposed to do. I wanted to toss him the phone like it was a hot potato, but before I could, the woman spoke again. "Clearly. Is my husband there?"

"Who?" I squeaked out.

"My husband," the woman demanded. "Nolan."

I'm sure my eyes were bugging out of my head when I turned to Clark to hand him the phone.

"Hello?" he answered. "What in the actual fuck?" he growled. "Have you lost your goddamned mind? Hold on."

Clark turned to me, pulling the phone away from his ear and placing it on speaker, clearly not caring that his wife had caught him in bed with another woman.

"She tell you she was my wife?" he asked. I wasn't sure who he was speaking to so I remained quiet until he added, "Reagan?"

I didn't want to speak so instead I nodded.

"You have. You've lost your mind telling my

woman that you're my wife. Bitch, I got shot of your cheating ass over a decade ago."

His woman? Did he tell her I was his woman?

"Nolan," she whined.

"Do not *Nolan* me. You have some balls calling my house. I have not one thing to say to you."

I didn't want to listen to this conversation; I started to get up, and Clark pulled me back to his side and pinned me with a stare.

"Well, I have something to say to you. I've been arrested, and unless you want your son to go into the system, you'll come pick him up."

Nope. I couldn't listen anymore. I was intruding on a private conversation; I was getting ready to bolt when the smallest of tremors started in Clark's hand. I watched as the phone shook in his hand and I didn't know what to do, but I knew what I couldn't do. No matter how uncomfortable I was, I couldn't abandon him.

"My son?" Clark whispered.

She hadn't heard or wasn't willing to repeat herself because his question was met with silence. Clark looked like he was ready to commit numerous acts of violence, the first being against the phone that looked like it was ready to be crushed in his hand.

No one was speaking, and I remembered she said she'd been arrested.

"Where are you?" I asked.

"I'm not speaking to you. Where's Nolan."

I instantly despised that she called him by his first name. No one else did, everyone else called him Clark, leaving me the only one in the privacy of his room to call him by that name. It was special. He'd told me to use his first name when we were intimate. This woman saying it made me want to wash her mouth out with soap and tell her never to say it again.

"He's getting dressed," I lied. "You're stuck talking to me. Where are you?"

"Hayward Police Department," she answered.

Hayward? I wasn't from around here and had only ventured out a few times, but I thought Emily and I went through a town called Hayward yesterday.

"Georgia?" I asked. I don't know why, but I'd thought she'd live in his home state of Nebraska, not here.

"Aren't you a smart one. This was my one call. Tell Nolan that if he doesn't want Nicholas in foster care, he better come down here and get him."

The small tremors had turned into violent shaking. Oh shit. I needed to end this conversation.

"Okay. Um. It takes about twenty minutes to get there. Is Nicholas at the police station with you?"

I wasn't sure if I should commit to picking the boy up. Surely Clark wouldn't leave his child at a police station to get taken by CPS, even if it was a child he didn't seem to know he had.

"No. The cops left the kid on the side of the road when they brought me in."

What a fucking bitch.

The kid? She called her son *the kid.* Who does that?

Clark remained quiet, and I didn't think it was my place to scold this craptastic mother so I, too, didn't say anything.

"Great. See you in twenty," I told her.

"You better not come. I called Nolan, not his side piece."

Clark was going to blow; the hold he had on his temper was rapidly deteriorating.

"You'll be lucky if I show up and not Clark. I have a feeling you'd be better off dealing with me at this point."

I pried the phone out of Clark's hand, disconnected the call, and slid out of bed.

I thought he was broken. He looked much like he did when he was in the middle of a nightmare.

Dead eyes.

Unseeing.

Fuck!

"Clark?"

14

Furious didn't begin to describe what I was.

For the second time in my life, Stephanie Clark had planted a nuclear bomb in my life and sat back to watch it explode, uncaring about the collateral damage she was inflicting. I actually believed she got off on it. That was part of why she'd always plotted and planned, playing a long game of deception, so when the truth came out, everyone suffered.

Nicholas.

Nick.

Fucking bitch.

Reagan's soft voice pulled me from my thoughts, and I watched as she started to pull on her clothes.

"You should go." Her eyes narrowed as she

buttoned her jeans. "Back to the guest room. Get some sleep." I added.

"Why?"

"Why?" I asked.

"Yes, Clark. Why? Why do you want me to go back to the guest room? Do you want privacy? Do you want to be alone because you're in shock? Do you still love her and you're hurt? Why are you pushing me away?"

I wasn't sure why I'd told her she needed to leave.

Except I did.

"I am out of my mind pissed, and I don't want you to see me lose my temper. The last thing I want to do is scare you."

"Lose your temper," she told me. "As long as you're not mad at me, you won't scare me."

Honesty. That's what this woman inspired. I couldn't hide a damn thing from her when around every turn she was there giving me truth and hope. Now was not the time to be pondering all the reasons why and how this woman had brought me to my knees. Warning bells were blaring, cautioning me to pull away from her, yet all I wanted was to run at her full-steam.

"Fuck," I yelled. "Fucking bitch. She cheated on me. With my brother. Nicholas."

I could barely get the words out without bile wanting to come to the surface.

"What?"

Reagan was already dressed, standing across the room waiting for me to follow her so I could go and pick up a son I never knew I had. A son that bitch had named after my brother.

How was this my life?

How was I supposed to face a child that by no fault of his own had been born into this fucked up mess and call him Nick?

"I caught them together when I came home from deployment. The bitch smiled when I yanked my brother out of my goddamned bed. She cried for *him* when I kicked his ass and tossed him out the door. And she blamed *me* when Nick's helicopter was shot down and he died. She said it was my fault for wishing him dead."

"Bitch!" she said.

By the time I had finished my story I was dressed and ready to leave, or as ready as one can be when they've come to learn they have a child.

We walked out to my Jeep, and I was halfway to

the police station before I realized that Reagan was in the truck with me. I didn't have to ask her to come; it was a foregone conclusion she'd be by my side. She also hadn't pitched a fit about some crazy person calling and claiming to be my wife just to be a bitch. And she hadn't run out the door when she heard I had a son. I wasn't sure what I was supposed to do with those realizations. I decided there was nothing to do but be grateful to have her strength and understanding.

Reagan didn't seem to mind the silence or try and fill it. She sat quietly and let me try and sort my head out, not that it was going to happen in the twenty-minute drive, but I appreciated it. I realized I hadn't asked Stephanie what she'd been arrested for or why she was in Georgia. After our divorce and Nick's funeral, which she insisted on attending, I hadn't spoken to her again. There was nothing left to say. Stephanie had announced graveside in front of all the mourners I'd wished Nick dead. She aired our dirty laundry in front of everyone; telling them I was a horrible husband and it was Nick who she'd loved. She was planning on leaving me to be with him – the love of her life.

Of course, she'd been drunk, and everyone was appalled by her outburst, but that was typical Stephanie. She was a selfish attention whore that was known for her out-of-control fits, especially if she wasn't getting her way. She put me through hell. The last eleven years without her had been bliss. Now it seemed I'd stepped back into the fiery pits of the underworld. The first time I'd barely escaped, now she was going to own me forever.

Fuck.

I parked the Jeep in the lot in front of the station, but as I pulled my keys out of the ignition something started to nag in the back of my mind.

"It doesn't make sense," I said.

"What doesn't?" Rea asked.

"She was drunk at my brother's funeral."

"Okay."

"It doesn't add up. None of it. My brother's funeral was two months after I found them together."

"Okay," she said, still not understanding.

"I had come home from a six-month deployment. Nick died two months later. That would've put her at least eight months pregnant with my child – drunk at a funeral. She had no belly at the time. Not to mention I saw her fully nude the night I caught them together. The image is forever burned into my brain. There was no way she was over six months pregnant. The boy cannot be mine. There's no way. Come to think of it, I hadn't touched her for at least a month or more before I'd left. Our marriage was over by then; the very sight of her repulsed me. The last thing I wanted was to fuck her."

"So, he's not yours. Do you think he could be Nick's or were there other men?"

Just like that, she believed me. There was no second-guessing or accusations; she simply took my word for it and moved on.

"I have no idea. I hadn't realized she'd been fucking my brother. I still couldn't tell you how long she'd been doing it."

"What do we do now?"

We.

Not *you*, but *we*.

"We're here. I should go in and at least ask if the boy is Nick's. I won't leave my family behind. If he's not, then I guess I'll help the kid find his real dad."

I didn't know what the fuck I was supposed to do. The only thing I knew for a fact was that Nicholas was not my son. The knowledge should've made me feel better, but it didn't. My gut was telling me that Nicholas was my nephew and the poor kid had been saddled with an evil bitch for a mother.

"You're a good man, Clark," Reagan told me and squeezed my bicep.

"You wouldn't think that if you knew what was going on in my head."

"But you haven't acted upon it or even said it out loud. I don't think I'd be as in control if I were in your shoes. Let's go get this done so we can get Nicholas taken care of."

We walked side-by-side to the glass doors of the station. When I grabbed the handle to pull open the door - Reagan grabbed my hand and held tight. Once we explained to the desk sergeant why I was there, we sat and waited - Reagan held tight.

When a uniformed officer came and got us and walked us back to the bullpen – Reagan held fast.

We sat, and the man explained that Stephanie had been arrested for drunk driving and possibly vehicular manslaughter if the couple she ran off the road didn't pull through. Both the driver and passenger had been flown from the scene. Through that all – Reagan held strong.

"Where's Nicholas Clark? Was he harmed in the crash?" Reagan asked.

"He is uninjured. There was no collision. The other car swerved to avoid a head-on crash with, Mrs. Clark. The driver lost control when he overshot the shoulder and flipped his car," Officer Landers explained.

"Christ," I muttered.

"Nicholas is in the Captain's office. He's a good kid. Like so many other children of alcoholics, he is more the parent than the child. I became increasingly concerned when an eleven-year-old knew words like drunk tank and bail."

"What can you tell us about him?" Reagan asked.

"What do you mean?" the officer asked.

"Stephanie's call tonight was the first I've heard about Nicholas. I didn't know she was even in Georgia."

Officer Landers flipped through a file and pulled out a sheet of paper. "Nicholas Brady Clark. Date of birth October 15th, 2007. Last known address 10235 North Street, Baylor, Nebraska. Father – Nicholas Brady Clark. Mother Stephanie Lynn Clark."

"Come again? Who is the father?" I asked.

"Nicholas Clark – deceased March 1, 2007," Officer Landers clarified.

"Bitch," Reagan muttered. "Stephanie told Nolan that Nicolas was his son."

"No. She said she was calling the boy's uncle to come and get him."

"Un-fucking-real. May I see her before I take Nicholas home?" I asked.

Nicholas, my nephew, not my son.

"She told you that?" the man asked.

Fucking bitch.

"Yep. After she told my woman, while we were in my bed, that she was my wife." I watched Reagan's cheeks pinken. Maybe I should've left out the bed part, but I was pissed, and he was a man, he'd understand. "Then she told me I had a son. Something that I thought was true until I got here and remembered one of the last times I saw her skank ass was when I pulled my brother outta my bed. She was butt-ass-naked and not six months pregnant, which she'd have to be if it was mine, considering my ass had been in Afghanistan for that long. So, after all of that, I'd like a word."

"I bet you do. I'll take you down."

"I'm thinking it's a good thing she's behind bars," Reagan mumbled.

"You'd be right."

"I'll wait here." Reagan smiled and unfolded her hand from mine.

"Thank you." I kissed her quickly on the lips, a peck, which left much to be desired. I wanted to properly thank her for the support she'd given me but now was not the time.

She tilted her head back to look up at me. "Always."

Always. I believed she meant that and another piece of heart came alive.

The officer made small talk as he walked me farther into the precinct to the hold cells. She hadn't been transferred from booking yet.

"I hope you understand I can't leave you alone with her," he said.

"Completely."

He pointed to the cell in front of me, and I was momentarily shocked. The woman holding onto the bars was not the same woman I'd married.

Stephanie might've always been a bitch, but she was a gorgeous one. This woman was not gorgeous. Forgetting everything I knew about her and the crimes she was being held on, physically there was nothing pretty about her. Dull brown hair, lifeless green sunken eyes, her skin had a greyish hue to it. Nothing. There was no trace of the woman I fell in love with.

"Hey, baby, I knew you'd come down to see me," she slurred.

How had I missed that on the phone?

"I'm not here to see you, Stephanie. I'm here to pick up the boy. You know, my nephew."

"Oh, come on. He should've been ours. He can be now that Nick is gone. Me and you and Nicky."

"Are you out of your fucking mind? I didn't want your ass before I left on that last deployment. I didn't want you when I came home, and I don't want you now. I only came down here to tell you face-to-face never to contact me again."

"What?" she screeched.

"You heard me. Lose my number, forget my name, and while you're at it change your last name back to Smith."

"Fine. Then you can't see Nick." I flinched, thinking about the nephew I had never met.

Landers cleared his throat. When I glanced in his direction, he mouthed *bullshit*.

"We'll see about that. I protect what's mine. I will go to the ends of the earth to make the boy safe, even if it's from you."

And for the first time, I realized that was the truth. I didn't need to meet the boy to know that I would do everything I could to protect him. I'd long ago forgiven myself for the angry words I'd spoken to my brother, but I'd wondered if I'd ever forgiven my brother for his betrayal? I realized now I had, and I would make sure his son was taken care of.

"Fuck you. Why are you always such a dick?"

she screamed. "Fuck you."

"That's the Stephanie Clark I know," I told Landers.

"Jesus. The beauty you have upstairs is a step up in all the ways that matter," he said, loud enough for her to hear. "Let's go get Nicholas so the three of you can go home."

As I walked back to the bullpen, I tried to calm my racing thoughts. It wasn't lost on me that I was more nervous about meeting an eleven-year-old boy than I was facing down a platoon of terrorists. Right as I got my heart rate under control, I saw Reagan talking to a little boy. Scratch that, the kid was no little boy, he was damn near as tall as her. When they turned to look at us, I had to suck in a breath. There was no denying that was my brother's son.

Fuck.

It was like going back in time twenty-five-years and seeing Nick.

"Nolan, this is Nicholas," Reagan introduced me when we approached.

"Nice to meet you, sir," Nicholas said.

I was speechless; the resemblance was uncanny. Even the boy's voice sounded like Nick's.

Jesus Christ, Nicholas was my brother reincarnated.

15

Clark continued to stare at his nephew, and the boy started to shift uncomfortably under the scrutiny. I was getting ready to shake Clark out of his stupor when he finally spoke.

"Yeah. You too." Then to the officer. "Is there anything I need to do before we leave?"

"No. Everything's been taken care of. Nicholas will have a court-appointed lawyer. I'd expect a call in a few days to arrange a meeting to go over temporary custody."

Thankfully nothing more was said about Stephanie or her charges in front of Nicholas. Officer Landers was spot on when he said that Nicholas had taken on the parental role. He knew way too much for an eleven-year-old. Clark was going to hit the roof

when he found out this was not the first time
Stephanie had been arrested, leaving Nicholas to go
into foster care until she got out. From what little
he'd said, it was normally for a few days.

"What do you say we get out of here? You
hungry?" Clark asked.

"I'm fine." He was lying. I'd heard the boy's
stomach rumble a few minutes ago. He'd pulled a
granola bar out of the pocket of his pants and took
one small bite before he wrapped it up and put
it back.

Pants that were filthy and looked like they'd seen
better days.

I hated Stephanie Clark.

"I'm starving. Mind if we pull through a Micky-
D's before we head back to Nolan's place?" I asked,
hoping that Clark would understand that Nicholas
needed food.

"Thanks for all your help officer." Clark turned
to Landers and shook his hand.

"Have a good evening," he replied.

I remained quiet on the walk to the Jeep. I wasn't
sure what was supposed to happen next.

"Hey, Nicholas?"

"Yes, ma'am."

I couldn't help but laugh.

"Kiddo, you don't have to call me ma'am. I appreciate the show of respect. But you can call me Reagan or Rea. Whichever you prefer is cool with me. What I was going to ask you is if there was anything we forgot back there. A coat, a phone, tablet, anything?" It was odd that we'd left without any of his personal belongings. I didn't know if eleven-year-old boys still had teddy bears, but surely he had something.

"No. I didn't have anything in the car."

If I thought Stephanie was a bitch before, now I thought she was a super bitch. Her child didn't have a coat, but she'd found time to get plastered.

She was the very definition of a C-U-Next-Tuesday.

Clark's teeth clenched, and he stalked toward his nephew, causing the younger boy to cower.

"A few things before we get home. Most important of those, I will never hurt you. I know you don't know me, and have no reason to believe me, but mark this bud, no one will ever hurt you again. You never need to flinch away from me. I'm sorry I didn't think to ask you this while we were still at the police station. Do you know who I am?"

Damn. Neither of us was very good at this kid thing.

"Yes, sir. You're my Uncle Nolan," he answered.

Clark studied him again, looking like he was a thousand miles away.

"Did your mom ever tell you that you look just like your dad?" Clark asked.

Oh shit.

"No. She never told me anything about him other than he was dead."

Clark recoiled at Nicholas' statement.

"Yeah. He is... umm... he died in a helicopter crash. Anyway, you look just like him. It's actually spooky how much, you even have his crazy-cool eyes. One green, one half green half brown. You're gonna have to bear with me a little if I keep staring at you. Honest to God I've never thought I'd see my brother again, but it's like he's standing in front of me."

I may have been wrong, but I could've sworn I heard a hitch in Clark's voice.

"Anyway. My friends call me Clark. I could imagine it would be a little weird if you called me that since it's your last name, too. But you can call me Nolan, uncle, hey you, basically anything other than sir. As Reagan said, I appreciate the respect, but you're my blood; you don't have to call me sir."

"Will you tell me about him? Mom got mad whenever I asked questions, so I stopped asking.

She'd always get really upset and drink more than usual if I brought him up."

"Sure. I can tell you about him sometime."

Oh, dear God, this was going to gut Clark. After what I'd learned tonight I didn't think Nick was his favorite person, Stephanie wasn't either, and how the hell was he supposed to explain that Stephanie had been his wife, not Nick's.

"So why don't you tell me the last time you ate," Clark asked.

"Other than the granola bar. A real meal," I quickly added.

"Yesterday morning."

"Christ. Alright, we'll hit a drive-thru tonight since there's nothing else open and we'll get some real food in you starting tomorrow."

"No. I'm fine really. I don't want to be a bother."

"Oh hell," I muttered, and Nicholas looked at me. "You're Nolan's family, sweetie. Family is never a bother."

"Come on. Let's get in the car. It's cold, and you don't have a jacket." Clark finished unlocking his Jeep.

I could tell by the tightness in his voice he hadn't liked Nicholas's comment any more than me.

We hit a drive-thru on the way home, and I

ordered a bunch of food that I knew Clark-my-body-is -a-temple didn't approve of, but the kid had to eat. There was no way Nicholas was going to bed hungry. Even if his belly was full of grease and empty calories – it was something.

I laid the food out on the dining room table, and Nicholas was giving a mound of fries side-long glances. I could practically see the saliva pooling in his mouth he wanted them so bad.

"Hey, kiddo, dig in. Eat whatever you want, as much as you want. I think my eyes are bigger than my stomach. I can't eat all of it on my own." Then I turned to Clark. "Nolan, can you help me?" I asked and walked down the hall.

Leaving the room was two-fold. I wanted Nicholas to feel free to eat, and I didn't think he'd do it while Clark and I watched. The other reason was I needed to talk to Clark in private.

"What's wrong?" he asked when we stepped into his bedroom.

"Nothing, other than the obvious. I actually wanted to check on you. This can't be easy."

He opened his mouth to lie to me, I was sure of it. He thought better and clamped it shut, grinding his teeth.

"Right. That's what I thought. You need to take a

minute to yourself. Go out front and have a smoke and get your thoughts together. I got Nicholas."

"I don't smoke in front of kids..."

"That's why I said out front. We won't be able to see you." I cut him off. "I don't mean to overstep, but he needs clothes. I'm supposed to help Emily tomorrow. Are you okay with me taking Nicholas with us? I'll hit the mall and pick him up some stuff."

"Christ," he said and ran his hand through his short-cropped hair. "I don't know what to do with a kid."

That admission took a lot out of Clark. He was used to being in complete control of his surroundings. He was so far out of his element it wasn't even funny. Hell, I was too.

"You'll figure it out. He's eleven, not two. At least he can wipe his own ass; I hear that stage is... yucky." I smiled, trying to interject something other than seriousness.

"I'd appreciate you taking him. I'll have to talk to the Commander tomorrow, and the team. I'm not sure what this will mean for me."

"Plenty of people have kids in the military. You'll work it out."

"No doubt about that. I'll leave the 707 before I

allow my nephew to go live with strangers because of my job instability."

I didn't understand what the big deal was. But Clark seemed to think there was one, so I'd take him at his word. I knew nothing about his job or the military for that matter.

"You got this. I know you do. Give it a week, and the two of you will be best-buds."

He chuckled and planted a kiss on my forehead that sent waves of electricity through my body. God, I loved when he touched me. It was going to totally suck when I had to leave. I could very easily get addicted to him. Who the hell was I lying to? I already was.

"Thank you. I couldn't have gotten through tonight without you."

"You would've, but you're welcome. Go take your time out, and I'm gonna talk to the kid. Feel him out a little and find out who his favorite band is. But you have to know, if you take too long, I'll have him over to the dark side listening to Tay-Tay."

Clark laughed a full belly laugh, and my heart soared.

I did that.

Fuck yeah!

"I'll be quick."

I stayed where I was for a minute and heard him mumble something to Nicholas, then the door shut. When I got back to the table, Nicholas had eaten one of the chicken sandwiches and was shoving a handful of fries in his mouth.

He was starving.

Not bothering to stop by the table, I walked to the fridge and opened it.

"Orange juice, almond milk – gross by the way, or water?" I asked.

"I'm fine," he answered.

I glanced at him, and he was looking at me like he had something to say. I decided not to say anything and wait him out. Instead, I pulled out two bottles of water and sat them at the table, placing one in front of him.

My patience paid off. "Are you his girlfriend?"

Well, I'd thought it paid off, but that was not what I thought he was going to ask.

"Nope. We're just friends. I live in Florida and Clark was nice enough to let me stay here."

"Am I going to live here?"

Shit. Not only did I not know the answer to that, but I was also not the person to be talking to him about family stuff.

"Do you want to?" I asked, instead of answering.

"Yes. No. I don't know. It's better than a group home or staying with strangers."

"I can understand that."

I couldn't. I'd never been in foster care or a group home.

"Who will take care of my mom if I stay here?"

Stupid bitch!

"She'll take care of herself, sweetie. Your uncle will work that out."

"She can't. I have to."

"If you take care of her, then who takes care of you?" I asked, gently afraid of the answer.

"I do."

That's what I thought he was going to say. Eleven, and he was taking care of himself. Disgraceful.

"You don't have to worry about that anymore. Clark will handle everything."

"But mom said that he didn't like me; that's why he never came around."

"She lied," I told him, then almost instantly regretted my words. "What I mean is, Clark didn't know about you." I smiled at him. "Nicholas, I want you to listen to me. If your uncle knew about you, you would've known him. There would've been nothing that would've kept you from him. I promise you that's the truth."

"Bud?" Clark said from across the room, startling us both. I hadn't heard him come in and I was pretty sure neither had Nicholas. "There's a lot that you're too young to know; some I will never tell you, and some I will explain when you're older. One thing I can tell you now is this – the last time I saw your mom was the last time I spoke to her, and she did not tell me she was pregnant with you. I'm sorry that I didn't know."

Nicholas didn't say anything, but he had understood what Clark said and was mulling it over.

"Do you want me to live here?" Nicolas asked.

"Yes." Clark's answer was strong and resolute, leaving no room for doubt. "We'll work things out together. When the lawyer calls, we will meet with her together. Me and you. One step at a time. Rea is going to take you to the mall tomorrow to pick you up some clothes. Are you okay going with her and our friend Emily?"

"Yeah. But the Goodwill is fine."

I was all for the Goodwill. I loved second-hand shops. I always found killer deals there, but anger was bubbling up. Stephanie could keep herself in liquor yet wouldn't spot for a new pair of jeans for her boy. That was jacked. Big time.

"We will for sure hit some consignment shops and the Goodwill, too. But you're gonna need some shoes and some other stuff that the mall will be better for."

"Okay. If it's not too much trouble."

I stood and ruffled his mop of brown hair then replaced my hand with a quick kiss. "No trouble at all. It will be fun. Your uncle is at work all day, and I get bored. It'll be cool to hang out with you."

"I'm going to get myself out of the guest room. Is it cool if I put my bag in your room?" I asked Clark when I walked by.

"Absolutely."

I made quick work cleaning up the room I'd stayed in and dumped my stuff in Clark's room. After I told the men it was ready for Nicholas, and I was going to wash up for bed, I used Clark's master bathroom to wash my face and brush all the french fry grease from my mouth. I was pulling on a pair of sweatpants when Clark walked in. No, he didn't walk, he prowled toward me and without a word his hands were in my hair and his mouth was on mine.

He pushed us back into the bathroom, keeping a tight hold on my hair. I was impressed when he shut and locked the door, shoved my sweats down, and placed me on the countertop - all without breaking the kiss. The zipper of his pants rasped, and I opened my legs to give him more room. He stepped closer and stopped.

"Are you on birth control?" he asked, then licked the shell around my ear.

"Yeah."

My answer had barely been verbalized before he pushed his dick inside of me, bottoming out. I didn't have time to catch my breath before his lips were back and he'd set a furious pace.

I wasn't sure where his desperation came from, and I didn't care. He'd quickly built a raging inferno, and I was eager for the explosion that was just out of reach. I tilted my hips and the added friction was exactly what I needed. Clark swallowed my cries and joined me in all-consuming pleasure.

When he brought his gaze up to meet mine, my heart nearly broke. He didn't try and mask his pain. There in his bathroom he gave me the greatest gift – his truth. He didn't hide anything, nothing was withheld as he stared into my eyes. I didn't need him to tell me with words that finding out his brother had a son was killing him. Knowing Nicholas pretty much had a shit life was going to eat at him. How could it not?

Clark gently cleaned me and carried me to his bed, setting me on the side. I scrambled back and used my oversized shirt to cover my lady bits.

"Should I sleep on the couch?" I asked.

Before the drama with Stephanie, we hadn't exactly firmed up sleeping arrangements, and now there was a child in the house.

"No. I want you in my bed."

I didn't think that was the best idea, but his answer didn't leave much room for argument. Sleeping next to him seemed more like a relationship than fuck-buddies.

"Alright." I agreed and moved over.

He settled in and pulled me close, cuddling his front to my back, spooning.

"If you feel me moving or starting to have a nightmare, promise me you won't touch me, and you'll get out of bed."

"I promise."

"Night, baby."

Baby? Sweet Jesus I was never going to recover.

"Good night, Nolan."

I love you was on the tip of my tongue. Not completely, but dangerously close.

16

My hard-on was throbbing on Reagan's naked ass, and I was using ample amounts of self-control not to take her. After I'd awoken and the memories of last night flooded my mind, I couldn't do it. I'd taken her on the counter of my bathroom roughly and without thought of how she would feel about it. It was a dick move, and to make matters worse, I did it without a condom. I knew I was clean, and I wasn't worried about her medical history - more her mental care. I hadn't even asked, I took.

Something new to add to the list of all the ways this woman makes me lose my mind. I'd planned on going slow; I just wanted to feel her. Then the impulse to claim her washed over me. Once the urge had taken root, all I wanted was to own every part of her. She was remarkable. Drama on top of drama was thrown at her last night, and she handled it all – without complaint. It was more than that; she'd simply stepped up and stood by my side, some of the time she took the lead, realizing I was ready to lose my shit.

Stephanie strikes again.

Stephanie Clark had always been a disaster but this? This shit was beyond compare. How could any mother put their child through what she had? I didn't know the half of it, and I was afraid I didn't want to know the rest. I couldn't believe that bitch told Nicholas that I didn't like him. I was lost and man enough to admit it. My job, raising a kid, repairing the damage that viper had inflicted, Reagan. I was in over my head on all accounts.

"What has you thinking so hard back there?" Reagan's sleep rough voice made me smile.

"What makes you think I'm thinking?" I quipped.

"I hope that's what has your attention and you're already not bored with me."

She wiggled her ass against my cock, and I groaned.

"How do you feel?" I asked, positioning myself at her opening, teasing the entrance with the head.

"Magnificent." She giggled.

"You good if I go bareback?" I asked.

"Yes." She pushed back, forcing the tip to slip in.

My hand snaked under her shirt and pushed it up, exposing her back to my lips and breasts to my hands.

"You have great tits, baby."

I couldn't keep my mouth off her skin. I wasn't picky. As long as I could kiss, lick, or suck her silky flesh, I was in heaven. Reagan's pants turned into moans, and the bucking of her hips became urgent when I pinched and pulled on her nipples.

"Catch up, Nolan, I want you to come with me."

Shit. I almost came as soon as the demand left her mouth.

"Bossy this morning. I should draw this out. Make you wait to take your pleasure." She reared back, taking me so deep my balls tightened, and my eyes slammed shut. "Fuck. Come with me, Rea. Now baby."

We both moaned together and fell over the edge. When my mind cleared enough to think, I realized another piece of the puzzle had clicked into place.

Nicholas was sitting eating pancakes that Reagan had made him before she scurried off to get ready.

"What grade are you in, bud?" I asked.

I knew absolutely nothing about the kid and only after Reagan said he'd need school supplies did I even contemplate what it would mean to get him enrolled. She laughed her ass off when she'd asked how good the school system was in my area and I had no idea what that meant.

"Sixth," he answered between bites.

"Do you like school? Get good grades?"

He washed his mouthful of food down with a gulp of orange juice and answered, "When I'm there I do. I don't get good grades because I miss most of the tests."

I knew what that meant. Stephanie was too drunk or hungover to drive him there. The woman was unreal.

"We'll have to start looking into enrolling you in school after this weekend. Rea said that you guys could pick up some school supplies today too, or you can wait until I don't work and I can take you."

"I don't want to be a bother."

There was that word again. I was beginning to

despise that word. No child should ever feel like they're a bother or burden.

I took my coffee and sat across from him. "Look at me bud." He did, and I had to force myself to hold his gaze. It was painful to look at him - a mini version of my brother. "Please stop saying you don't want to be a bother. You are not one. Whether you live here for the long haul or not, this is your home. Wherever I am, wherever I live, you will always be welcome. You do not ask for permission to get something to eat or drink; you help yourself. It's yours. That bedroom is yours. The TV, the movies, all yours. Make yourself at home."

I'd have to remember to check my movies, not that I had many DVDs. Most of my collection was digital but the movies that were not kid-friendly needed to be moved.

"I'd like to go get school stuff with you," he answered, then added "I didn't see a chore list. Do you have one for me?"

"A chore list?"

"In the group homes, there's always a list of stuff that each person has to do, you know, to earn their keep."

Motherfucker.

"You don't earn your keep. This is your home.

Remember? I'll make you a deal. You keep your room straight, and if I need help around the house, I'll ask. But while we're working out the kinks, how about you sit back, relax, and get used to me and your new house. You'll start school, have homework, stuff you'll need to concentrate on."

"Okay."

"Are you still hungry?" He didn't answer but looked at his plate. "One more thing. I want the truth. I'll always be honest with you and, in return, I want the truth from you – always."

"Yes, I'm still hungry."

"Good. Check the pantry and fridge and tell me what you want."

He did as I asked, giving me the opportunity to look at him. He was tall but skinny, too skinny.

There was a knock on the door before I heard it open and Jasper waltzed his ass into my house. He had a habit of entering dwellings without permission.

"This isn't Lenox's house. Don't make a habit of barging in," I scolded, even though I wasn't angry.

"Right. Because you might be banging..."

"Don't finish that." I stopped the crude comeback.

"Crap. Forgot," he apologized.

"Hey bud, come here. I want to introduce you to my friend."

Nicholas walked in, eyed Jasper with suspicion, and stepped closer to me.

While it felt good that he'd come to me for protection, I was pissed he thought he had to. This was his house, and he damn well should feel safe in it. Another thing I'd talk to him about.

"Yo. Nicholas, right?" Jasper gave him a chin lift.

"Yeah, but everyone calls me Nick."

My heart flipped, and I hoped I was able to cover it before he saw.

"Cool. So, Nick, you gonna hang out with the women today?" Jasper carried on.

"Yeah, Rea said we were going to the mall." The look that passed over Nick's face was clearly one of displeasure. I didn't blame the kid; I hated shopping too.

"Sorry, kid. That sucks. Maybe this weekend you can hang with the guys, and we can toss a ball or something."

"Really?"

"Absolutely. My boy Jason would love to hang out too. He's a little younger than you, but he's pretty good at football. Do you like to play?"

"I've never played football," Nick answered.

"We'll have Levi come along too. He was the star quarterback at his high school. Maybe he can teach you a thing or two since your uncle's still learning himself." Jasper chuckled at his joke, and I barely refrained from flipping him the bird.

"Can we?" Nick turned to me and asked.

"Of course," I answered.

Reagan came into the room, and I wanted to haul her ass back into my room. I had no idea how she'd managed to get into the jeans she was wearing. They were tight, sexy as hell, and showcased her tight ass. Hot damn!

"What'd I miss?" she asked.

"Nothing. Guys making plans," Jasper told her.

"Uncle Nolan, is it alright if I have a bowl of cereal?"

I stopped myself from correcting him, remembering it would take time for him to feel comfortable.

"You need help?" I asked instead.

"No."

"Then help yourself. Jasper and I are going to head to work now. You good?"

"Will you be home tonight?" he asked.

"Yeah. I'll be home around five," I assured him and wondered if there were times that Stephanie didn't come home, leaving him to fend for himself.

"I left you a card on the counter," I told Reagan, bending to give her soft kiss on her lips before continuing. "Thanks for your help."

"Of course. Have a good day at work," she whispered.

"Please settle Emily down today; she's having a shit hemorrhage." Jasper's brows were pulled together, clearly unhappy about Emily's state of mind.

Reagan easily agreed to talk to Emily and check in later.

We were halfway to work before Jasper spoke. "Seems like things have changed between you and Reagan."

It was a statement, one I was going to ignore. Things had changed, only I wasn't sure they were for the better. Yet again, Stephanie had fucked with my life, turning everything on its head at the blink of an eye. She did have the worst timing. Not that finding out about Nicholas wasn't welcomed, even if it was eleven years late. I only had a limited amount of time left with Reagan, and now it was going to be filled with lawyers, schools, and a boy that was going to need more of my attention than I had hours in the day.

Maybe it was time to cut her loose. The last thing

Reagan needed was having to deal with the fallout from my ex-wife. I filled Jasper in on last night, and when I was done, he had the same what-the-fuck look I had last night.

"You know we'll all pitch in and help where we can," he said.

""Preciate it."

17

"Let's go. Let's go," Nick nagged.

Clark chuckled, and I rolled my eyes – for the tenth time today.

Nick had settled in nicely. It'd taken a few days, but after the court-appointed attorney and the social worker came to the house and explained that Clark would be granted temporary guardianship, Nick seemed to relax. The conversation about Clark applying for custody of Nicholas had also been discussed. When Nick started fidgeting and expressing concern about who would take care of Stephanie, Clark stopped the conversation and told the attorney that permanent custody would be filed when Nick was ready.

"Uncle Nolan," he whined again. "Make her hurry up."

"You don't rush a woman when she's getting ready," Clark answered.

I could hear them moving around the living room when I grabbed my sneakers and headed down the hall. We were going to Jasper's to play catch in their backyard again. We were supposed to meet at the park this time so the guys could have more room, but Emily changed the plans at the last minute.

"Why's that?"

"Because, when a beautiful woman cares enough about you to take her time to look nice, you appreciate it. That and she might take your head off if you rush her."

Nick laughed at his uncle. He'd been doing more of that lately, and it was a pleasure to watch.

"Ha-ha. Funny guy today. Well, if you jokesters are done messing around, let's hit the road."

I caught Nick making a face at Clark, and my heart swelled. I loved that the two of them were getting close. Nick was a great kid. It was going to be hard to leave. We hadn't talked about how quickly the week had passed and how fast the day was approaching when I'd be going to Florida. The three of us had been living in a bubble.

Much to Clark's dismay, Nick and I took over the radio as soon as we got into the Jeep and by the time we were pulling into Jasper's driveway he was threatening to cancel his satellite radio subscription if we ever used the Top-100 station again.

Secretly, I think he liked the music. More than once I caught him strumming his sexy fingers on the steering wheel as he maneuvered down the highway. What was it about a man driving that was so sexy? Every time we got in the Jeep I wanted to crawl into his lap and wedge myself between the steering wheel and his hard chest or lean over the center console and give him the blowjob I've wanted to try but had yet to work up the courage to do.

How exactly was one supposed to approach that topic? *Hey Clark, I've never given head, mind teaching me? By the way, I apologize in advance if I bite your dick in the process.* Ouch. I bet he'd jump right on that and let me use his member for practice. Maybe I should start with a piece of fruit, see if I can manage that without bruising the peel before I move on to a real-life penis.

"What are you thinking about that has your face so red?" Clark whispered in my ear.

I hadn't realized we'd stopped and he'd turned off the car. Oops.

"Nothing," I squeaked.

"Hey, bud. Do me a favor, yeah? Go into the house and tell Jasper we'll be right there."

Nick jumped out without complaint or question and ran for the door.

"Tell me." Clark kissed the skin around my throat, sending chills to all the right places. "Tell me." He continued his exploration up to my earlobe and sucked it into his mouth. "Tell me."

"Oh, all right. I was thinking about how I've never given a blowjob and was wondering what my chances were of you teaching me."

Embarrassed was an understatement. I needed to learn how to shut up.

"Let me get this straight. You want me to teach you how to suck me off, and you thought I'd say no?"

"I could bite you. Or not be any good at it."

"You planning on biting me?" His eyebrows lifted, punctuating his question.

"Of course not."

"Then I can tell you that it will be good."

"How do you know that? I've never done it before."

Clark framed my face with his large hands, pulling me close before he answered. "Baby, nothing could be bad about you taking my cock in your mouth. Just the thought of it is getting me hard. If you did nothing more than use your pretty pink tongue to lick it, I'd still shoot off."

"Can I try it tonight?"

Could I sound anymore eager?

"Feel free to try anytime you'd like."

The house was full of people by the time we'd made our way inside. I looked around noticing that Lily and Blake were both absent.

"Where's Lily?" I asked Emily, remembering she was almost ready to give birth.

"She went to rest in my bed, said that she was having a few contractions but didn't want Lenox to know. And Blake is at the Post today working on some issue the guys ran into this week," she answered.

"Shouldn't Lily go to the hospital?"

"No." Emily laughed. "The contractions aren't regular; she's been having them for days. She's not due for another two weeks."

The mention of Lily's due date reminded me that I would miss the birth of the baby. Both Lily and Lenox knew the sex of the baby, but they'd refused to tell anyone. I thought it was cool they had their own little secret, but it was driving the rest of the guys crazy.

"How are you feeling?" Last time I saw Emily she thought she was getting the flu but looked a lot better today.

"I'm... um... I don't have the flu," she stuttered.

"Well, that's good."

"Let's get the guys out back to play catch, and we'll talk," she whispered.

We still hadn't found a new venue for Jasper and Emily's wedding, and the ordeal was taking a toll on her. Last night on the phone she revealed she was still worried it was the universe's way of keeping them apart. I hadn't had the chance to tell Jasper what Em had told me. He will lose his ever-loving-mind when I tell him. One thing was certain; he loved Emily and Jason more than I've ever seen a man love his woman. He wouldn't want her upset or sad for one minute. I had faith that he'd assuage her fears.

The men quickly dispersed to the backyard at Emily's suggestion, and we watched through the back window as they picked teams and huddled together.

"I'm pregnant," Emily announced.

"What?"

"I'm scared to death," she went on. "When Jasper came back from visiting you in Montana, we'd talked about the possibility of kids in our future. We both agreed we wanted them, but he was clear that he didn't want it to happen until we were married. Now, here I am pregnant and I can't find a damn place to marry us."

"You think he'll be mad?" I asked, or afraid he'll run like he did with my sister. I didn't ask the last part out loud. Part of the reason was it was plain old rude, even with my lack of social grace I knew that. The other part was I was afraid of her answer. I knew Jasper wouldn't leave her, and truthfully somewhere deep down inside that hurt. It shouldn't, but it did.

"I don't know."

"Emily, listen to me. He won't be mad. He's going to be thrilled. He won't care for one second you're not married. Jasper loves you with all his heart."

"Damn right I do," Jasper said. "What's wrong?"

Both of us startled at his intrusion; I hadn't heard him come in. I remained silent. This wasn't my secret to tell. If Emily wanted to wait to tell him when their house wasn't full of people; I couldn't blame her.

"Nothing," she said, but she wasn't fooling anyone with the hitch in her voice.

"Emily." Jasper's declaration left no room for her to sidestep this conversation. Crap.

"I'm pregnant," she blurted out.

And here people say that I was blunt and just said whatever popped into my head. It was the truth, I did do that, but Emily didn't try and lead into her announcement in any way. She just ripped the Band-Aid off. Much to Jasper's credit, his face remained blank for a moment before his lips curled up into a smile.

"Yeah?" he asked.

"Yeah," she confirmed.

"We're gonna have a baby," he said rhetorically.

"You're not mad?"

"Fuck no. How could I be mad that my beautiful, sweet wife is having our baby?

"But I'm not your wife," she reminded him.

I didn't need to be a part of this private moment; I didn't *want* to be a part of it. I was thrilled to pieces they were going to have a baby, but the memories of my sister's pregnancy were stirring in my mind. How scared she was, how lonely, how strong she'd been going through it all by herself. It was water under the bridge, and I'd never bring it up to Jasper. Liz loved Jasper the way only a best friend could love. She forgave him and understood his reaction. Jasper had finally freed himself of the guilt and pain that had eaten away at him for years. No way would I ever want those feelings to return. He deserved to be happy and have a family.

"I don't need some damn piece of paper to tell me that you're my wife..."

I slipped out the back door while Jasper was in mid-sentence. The heat of the day blasted me in the face, hot and humid, so different than the weather in Montana. Florida was going to be even worse. I'd need to junk half my wardrobe, exchanging it for climate appropriate clothes. I'd have time before my new job started and luckily the office I would be working in was casual. Hell, when the owner interviewed me he was in cargo shorts and a polo. I'd only need what would be considered office attire when I went on-site to meet with clients.

I watched the men patiently tossing the football with the younger boys, stopping to give them instruction every now and then. Levi was showing Nick how to achieve the perfect spiral when throwing the ball, and Clark was explaining the proper way to catch then tuck the ball so as not to fumble.

I was going to miss this, miss them all. Most of all I was going to miss Clark and Nick. My heart ached at all the things I wouldn't be here for - Lily's baby being born, Jasper's wedding, Emily's pregnancy, Clark learning how to be a parent and uncle. I'd fallen in love with both Clark and Nick. He warned me not to; told me in no uncertain terms he did not want a relationship and what we had together was nothing more than fun. But it felt like more. He kissed me before he left the house every day. We slept cuddled together like a pile of puppies, touching as much as humanly possible. He showered with me and washed my hair. He'd told me about his family and the brother he once loved and adored until Nick had betrayed him in the worst way. He'd even told me how he met Stephanie and what their life had been like when it was good. He took the blame for his marriage going bad – deployments, workups, training – he'd explained all the time he'd been away took its toll on her. She needed and wanted attention he couldn't give her. I wasn't sure how that gave her a free pass to cheat on him, but he took responsibility for not being the man she needed. It was not his fault she was a selfish attention whore, but there was no changing his mind.

"What are you thinking about?" Clark pulled a chair closer to mine and sat, chugging down a bottle of water. My thighs clenched at the sight of his biceps flexing as he held the bottle to his lips.

"I have an announcement," Jasper's voice boomed, cutting off my answer.

Thank God! Knowing me I would've told him the truth, causing Clark to run a mile. Which would've been for the best, but I wasn't ready to lose him yet. The time was coming fast enough.

"Jason, come here bud."

Jason ran to Jasper and he leaned down to whisper something to him. Jason's eyes were huge and his smile was even bigger. "Really?" he asked. Jasper nodded and turned to the rest of us.

"Emily's having my baby."

His proclamation brought about hooting and high-fives. There were hugs and back pounding going around, and I prayed I could mask my heartache. This was what I'd wished for my sister when she found out she was pregnant.

Clark's fingers threaded through mine, and he squeezed as though he could read my thoughts. I was grateful for his support, but it only made me feel worse. I was a horrible person. This wasn't about me or Liz or what'd happened in the past. This was a celebration of life – of love. I plastered on a smile and hoped it would hide the turmoil that was swirling in my stomach.

Blake had finished her work in time to join us to

eat. Once she got there, she'd made her way to Levi's side and never moved. She smiled at him like he'd hung the moon and I suppose in her universe he had. The love they shared was almost unbearable to watch. I could lie to myself all I wanted, but the truth was, I wanted that. Lily came down from her nap feeling better, yet Lenox still insisted she sit down and waited on her hand and foot. I wondered if that was how Jasper was going to be with Emily? I hoped so. She deserved that and knowing Jasper the way I did, I was sure he'd give it to her.

Clean up was done and we were once again in the backyard sitting around watching Nick and Jason pass the ball to each other using the new skills they'd learned today. Little Carter was running back and forth between them trying to get the ball. However, at almost two, he was too small to actually catch the ball, not that he seemed to care. He'd squeal in delight anytime the ball was dropped, and he could pick it up and run with it.

Yeah, I was going to miss this.

I'd had a lot of friends in Montana but never a close-knit circle like this. We didn't barbeque at each other's houses and share a bond like this group did. Moving was going to suck. I didn't think I'd ever find this again; friendships that were based on loyalty and history.

"Blake and I have something to tell you," Levi started. "We only found out, but after Jasper's announcement, we've decided to tell you all now. Blake's...um..." Levi took a moment to gather his composure. "She's pregnant too."

If I'd thought the celebration Jasper and Emily had received was loud, Levi's was ten-fold. The group was animated and energetic at the announcement of another baby. Two in one day.

"Never would've guessed," Lenox said. "A few years ago, I thought we were all happy doing what we loved. The thought had never crossed my mind that there was more. And I really didn't think that there'd be kids involved. Happy for you both."

The other guys agreed, all smiling at each other when Lily spoke up.

"When I met you all, you were like a wild pack of dogs." She laughed.

"Two more little ones to welcome to the family," Emily smiled.

"We better make that three," Lily said, and everyone looked at her not understanding. "My water just broke."

Everyone jumped into action except Lenox. He remained seated by his wife, smiling at her.

"You ready?" he asked.

"Yeah. Piece of cake. Push another watermelon out of my vagina."

"Damn, you make me want to rush out and get knocked up so I can experience that," I quipped and immediately regretted my joke. Clark's stare was heavy, and he looked pissed. I was going to explain what I'd meant and reassure him I was not, nor was I trying to become preggo, but stopped myself. I tended to get myself in more trouble with my explanations.

"Let's go have our boy." Lenox kissed Lily's forehead and helped her stand.

"A boy?" I asked.

Lily laughed and shook her head. "I'm surprised you didn't let it spill before now."

"Congrats, brother," Clark said, shaking Lenox's hand.

We all helped them to Lenox's truck and waved as they headed to the hospital to welcome son number two into the world. As planned, Emily and Jasper were keeping Carter for a few days so Lily and Lenox could have some time alone with the new baby.

"Let me know if you need any help with him," I told Emily as we were leaving.

Clark and Nick were already in the Jeep waiting for me, no doubt bitching about how long I take to say goodbye.

"I'm good. Thanks for everything." Emily hugged me and went inside, leaving me with Jasper on the front stoop.

"I know, Rea."

"You know what?" I asked.

Oh hell, was he going to tell Clark I'd fallen in love with him? He'd better not. I'd castrate him if he ruined my last few days.

"I know this is hard for you. The baby." Please God, don't let him go on. I didn't want to have this talk. "I wish they were here. I wish I'd done everything differently. I wish I wasn't such a fucking coward. I will take those regrets to my grave. I need you to know that I loved Liz and I wish that I could've given her everything she deserved. Alesha is my first child. I haven't forgotten her. Jason may not be my blood, but he is my son. My second child. When this baby comes, I will love it no more than I do my first two. I need you to know that."

"I know. I'm happy for you. Please don't go back down that road again letting guilt consume you.

There is a new life coming into the world, and it should be celebrated. Don't make room for the darkness and sadness of the past. Emily, Jason, and this new baby are your family."

"They are. But you're my family too. Liz and Alesha are still my family."

I needed to hear that more than I knew I did. My sister and niece hadn't been pushed aside and forgotten.

"Thank you. I appreciate it. I'm so happy for you both."

"I wish you lived closer. Jason is going to miss his Aunt Rea. And the new baby, too. He'll need you to spoil him."

"Him." I laughed.

"Have you seen my wife? God would not punish me with little girls with black hair and blue eyes. There is not enough ammo to keep little fuckers away." Jasper's smile faded when he'd realized what he'd said.

"You're dumb." I playfully slapped his chest, interjecting humor, not wanting him to feel bad. "Has it ever occurred to you that Emily would feel the same about little boys? I remember you in high school. All the girls swooned over you. I personally didn't see it, you were just Jasper to me, but I heard the girls talking about how hot you were." I made a gagging sound and Jasper smirked. "Do you think Emily wants to chase the girls away for her boy if he looks like you? She'll need a bat and a shotgun because any Walker boy is gonna be smokin' hot like his daddy."

There was a distinct growl behind me, and Jasper threw his head back and laughed.

"Christ, that is perfect," Jasper said.

I didn't see the humor in my current situation. Clark had once accused me of being in love with Jasper, and hearing me say that Jasper was smoking hot, even in a roundabout way out of context, he wasn't going to be happy.

"Ass," I whispered.

Jasper sobered and looked over his shoulder. "Life's funny. Just when you think you have it all figured out, you realize you don't. There you are chugging along and next thing you know your life is turned upside down and derailed. Situations, people, obstacles are thrown into your path. Do you sidestep them, plow through them, or embrace them? You taught me to embrace them, hold on, not let anything get in my way of happiness. I hope you can take your own advice."

I was thoroughly confused by Jasper's statement.

I didn't know if his words were meant for me or Clark. He hadn't moved his gaze from over my shoulder, but I didn't know what he was looking at. Maybe he was staring off into space lost in his thought. I didn't think so, but it was possible. He wasn't stupid, and he'd known me for a long time. I was sure he knew I was head over heels in love with Clark. Only there was nothing I could do about it; Clark didn't want me, and I wasn't going to make him feel bad for sticking to our arrangement. None of this was his fault. I didn't have the option to embrace and hold on like Jasper had suggested. The only thing I could do was sidestep my feelings and plow through the heartache. I did this. I'd fucked up and fallen in love with a man that was unavailable. I had to let go.

Life sucked.

18

She left.

Reagan was gone. I was miserable, and a little pissed even though I didn't have a right to be. We'd agreed - hell it was my idea, orgasms. Nothing but orgasms. Then why did I feel like my heart had been ripped from my chest and now resided in Florida?

The night before she left we all went to Lenox and Lily's for dinner. With Ethan being just home from the hospital, Lenox refused to take him in public for a goodbye party for Reagan. Everyone laughed and had a good time. As the hours had ticked by, my temper rose. She'd been smiling and happy, not a care in the world she'd be leaving the next morning. Even before that she'd started to pull away from me. I'd wake up in the morning, and instead of our bodies being tangled together, she was on the other side of the bed facing away from me. It shouldn't have pissed me off, but it did. I should've been happy that she was leaving with her heart intact and not hurt by our time together, but I wasn't.

That night when we got home, after Nick had gone to bed, I took her back to my room and unsuccessfully tried to show her what she meant to me, using my body to tell her all the things I couldn't verbalize. We each took our time exploring. I'd taken the time to memorize the feel of her body and the sounds she made. I'd allowed myself to embrace every emotion as it was happening. I made love to her slowly, sweetly. And the next morning she smiled, gave me a hug thanking me for letting her stay at my house, and cried when she said goodbye to Nicholas.

She gave me the brush off and a half-hearted promise to call. It had been a week and she hadn't. I knew she'd made it to her new apartment safely because she'd texted. I also got a short message when she started her job, telling me she loved it down in Florida and her co-workers were great. I couldn't help but be jealous. Did she work with men? Was she going on dates? She was fucking gorgeous; it wouldn't take long for those vultures to circle around her.

Jasper, Emily, even Lily had all talked to her on the phone and happily reported that she was doing great and having fun. Jasper was a pain in my ass passing me his phone when Reagan had texted him a picture of her on the beach. It was obviously a selfie with the caption, *why didn't I do this sooner?* The fucker smirked when I stomped out of the hangar for some fresh air. Sooner? What the hell did that mean? She wished she'd never stopped over in Georgia and spent time here?

The morning in my bedroom when I had Reagan pushed up against my door, I never thought I'd be the one to have fallen in love and she'd happily prance out of my life unscathed. When I carefully explained to her that I could only offer her a few nights, never did I imagine I'd want a lifetime. I guess I was too convincing and she'd taken me at my word.

Good for her, I didn't want her sad. Bad for me, I was in hell.

There was so much going on with Nick. I thought getting things straight would take all my time, but I still found time at night, when I fell into the bed I'd shared with Reagan, to contemplate how much I missed her. Nick did too. He talked about her all the time; it was salt in my wound. He'd go on and on and laugh about all the crazy shit she did. The girl had no shame. She'd gone out of her way to make Nick feel at home, dancing and singing around the house even though she couldn't carry a tune in a basket and her rhythm was a little off. She still did it, knowing that Nick thought it was funny and he'd laugh at her. So damn sweet.

"Do we have the drone footage yet?" Blake asked, reminding me I had work to do.

"Yes. I'll have it up on the big screen in a second," Levi answered his wife.

The rest of us gathered around when the screen flickered to life and the oil platform, Horizon III, came into view. The size of the rig was impressive. Blake had said it was a floating city and she hadn't been exaggerating. The image feed the drone had recorded was outstanding. Gone were the days of grainy pictures that needed to be enhanced; I could see the rust on one of the railings with great clarity.

"Damn. This is so much better than satellite," Jasper vocalized what I was thinking.

"What's that?" I asked. "Go back three frames." Levi did as I asked. "There." He quickly paused the video.

"We're looking at the top deck," Levi said. "Looks like supplies?"

"Is that a biohazard sticker on that box?" I asked.

Levi zoomed in and, sure enough, it was a red warning label.

"Why would there be biological material on an abandoned oil rig?"

"Fuck if I know. The box next to it..." Lenox pointed at the screen. "Has a logo on it can you get closer?"

Levi played the video in slow motion, waiting until we had a better view of the company name. Once the name became clear, Lenox had out his tablet looking the company up.

"Hospital medical equipment."

"If the rig was operational it wouldn't surprise me. The platform would have some emergency medical supplies. It is not exactly the safest environment to work in. Serious injury requires a medivac and we all know that can take too long," Blake explained.

"Equipment, not supplies. Anesthesia machines, cold chain equipment, Respolife." Lenox read a few more machines they sold on their website. "Anesthesia?" he asked when he was done.

"That doesn't make sense. I'll look into it, but I'd

think the only thing a rig medic would be worried about was stabilizing a patient, not putting them under." Blake scribbled something in her notebook and went back to watching the video.

By the time we were done, we had more questions than answers. Technically the team shouldn't have been looking into the rig; even though it was in international waters, it was in The Gulf. There also hadn't been any more chatter about eco-terrorists and explosives. The intel Blake had gathered should've been passed to Homeland or the FBI, either of them could've investigated, but Blake refused and asked us to back her with the Commander. She had a gut feeling that something was going on and the FBI wouldn't take it seriously. I'd learned to trust Blake. With the support of the team, the Commander agreed to allow us to continue to gather intel, but he wouldn't approve a mission until we had hard proof that national security was in jeopardy.

That worked for me just fine. I wasn't all that crazy to head on an op with Nick still getting used to living with me. He'd settled into his new school, he was making friends and seemed to like it. He was behind in his studies and I'd arranged a tutor for him. I thought he'd complain when I told him, but he was excited about not being the stupid one in class – his words, not mine. I had to step outside and curse in private after he'd made the admission. No kid should ever feel dumb, especially my nephew. The Commander had put me in contact with a wife of a Captain he knew. She was older and had been a teacher before she stopped working, preparing for her husband's retirement from the Army. She explained in a year from now I'd have to find someone else to help me with Nick because she and her husband were going to travel in their Winnebago.

Anna was a lifesaver, and Nick liked her. She picked him up from school and watched him until I got home. While she was there, they did his homework together, and the extra work the school had given him. She was a blessing, even starting dinner if I was running late.

The only snag Nick and I had was when he'd asked about his dad and wanted to see pictures of him. The issue had been on my part, not his, as we sat on the couch and I told him about my childhood with my brother, his father. It was painful remembering how close we'd been, all the memories I'd blocked once he'd betrayed me. I'd forgotten about the times Nick had followed me around with hero-worship. After I joined the Army, he'd followed there, too. He was a proud soldier and a good one. I'd known Nicholas was a dead ringer of Nick but seeing the pictures was uncomfortable and gut-wrenching. I wished Reagan was there with us as we went through the photo album. I couldn't explain why, but it felt like she should've been there.

Damn, I missed her.

19

I hated Florida.

My job was boring, but that could've been because my heart wasn't in it. Hell, my heart wasn't even beating in my own chest anymore. I'd left it back in Georgia along with the other half of my soul. Or was it my whole soul that I'd left? I was stupid, and over the last month, I'd reminded myself of that every morning I'd woken up. I thought it would get easier not seeing Clark or hearing his voice. That's why I'd refused to call him and only texted when I couldn't take the ridiculous ache any longer.

Like now, the radio was on, and I was getting ready for work. A Justin Bieber song came on, and all I could think about was Clark and his extreme distaste for the Biebs.

Me: Just thought I'd let you know that with the release of the new JB soundtrack you may be correct in your initial assessment of his musical ability. FLOP!

His reply was immediate.

Clark: I can sleep better at night knowing that you've seen the light.

I frowned when I read the message. Sleep? I couldn't remember the last time I'd had a restful night's sleep. Well, I could remember. It was the last night I'd slept tangled with Clark. After the night at Jasper's when Emily and Blake had announced their pregnancies, I'd stopped cuddling with Clark. After we'd make love... sex... it was sex; I had to keep reminding myself of that. After sex, I'd wait until Clark fell asleep then I'd roll over. It wasn't because I wanted the distance. It was the opposite; I wanted to curl into him and never let him go. I didn't want him for fun; I wanted him forever. But that's not what Clark had offered, so I rolled over, reminding myself he wasn't mine.

Me: Glad I can be of service. GTG. Getting ready for work. Have a good day.

Me: Be safe.

Clark: Always. Have a good day.

Always.

I wished we could have always.

Work sucked today. I had to go to the Alger Energy headquarters today, which required me to dress nicely. I was spoiled not having to wear heels to the office every day. Days like today when I had to suffer through a full day with my toes pinched into pumps; I cursed being a woman. I would be investing in a plethora of flats as soon as I could make time to get to the mall.

This project was taking all of my time. Even after office hours at home, I still had my laptop open and was working. Alger had two oil spills in the last two years. Not good. Their safety protocol had been called into question, and they were currently under review. One was an ocean spill costing the company millions in clean up; the other was a land spill. The tanker company was actually to blame, not the drill, but the media and OSHA didn't care. It happened on Alger property. That had cost less to clean up but was still costly. I couldn't imagine how the company hadn't folded after all the money they were bleeding.

Thankfully I didn't have to worry about their financial competence. My only job was to make them look good to the public. That's why I was at Alger HQ instead of my office. Lenard Glass, the new CEO, was meeting with me to go over all the philanthropic work the company did - the charities they gave to, the man hours they donated to the communities where they drilled. It was all smoke and mirrors. From my research, I'd found that Alger Energy raped the environment. They had the worst eco-stats in the industry which made me question why the EPA hadn't closed them down.

Sure, they gave money, they did clean up the messes they made, and they donated energy to other countries. But there had to be something hanky going on. A government payoff somewhere. Not that it was my business, merely an observation. One that made me feel kind of yucky for helping them with their public appearance.

"Good afternoon, Miss Reagan. A pleasure," Lenard cooed when he came into the cubicle I was given to use while at the office.

I hated that he called me, Miss Reagan. I'd asked him not to, but he'd ignored me. He'd also ignored me when I lied and told him I had a boyfriend when he asked me out. He was persistent and schwarmy.

"Hi, Lenard. What do you have for me today?"

The next few hours he combed through files, bragging about all the good deeds Alger Energy had done over the years. His grandfather had started the company, delivering propane and heating fuel in rural Texas. When Lenard's father, Lenard Sr., was old enough to join his father they had bought land that was oil-rich and started drilling. From there his father had bought more land, then started leasing oil platforms until the company could buy a small rig of their own. It was a great *rag to riches* story. Lenard's grandmother had died in childbirth, leaving Lenard Sr. to raise his son on his own. He never remarried, the story that had been passed down was one of true and lasting love. Lenard's grandfather had loved his wife so deeply she was irreplaceable. Somehow I doubted the story, but I'd use it in my campaign. Nothing worked better than pulling on someone's heartstrings, especially when dealing with an industry that was widely disliked.

I was relieved when Lenard's secretary called to tell him he was needed in a meeting. He'd rushed out, apologizing for his speedy exit, luckily forgetting to ask me to dinner for the twentieth time.

I was packing up to leave when I found a file he'd left on my desk. Rolling my eyes at his obvious attempt to make me see him again, I stowed it in my computer bag with the rest of my paperwork and left. I would've left it on the desk but some of the files he'd shown me had tax-exempt numbers in them, and I wasn't sure if those were like social security numbers and needed to be guarded. Just because I thought he was a little douchey didn't mean I wanted him or the company to fall victim to identity theft.

I forwent the office and headed straight home. The great thing about my job, my boss didn't care if I worked from home as long as the work was done. It was late enough in the afternoon I could ease my guilt of playing hooky by using midday traffic as an excuse.

It didn't take me long to finish my first draft of a series of press releases that would go out. My boss and I had gone over the PR strategy and decided press releases would be a great way to start before moving to the broader marketing campaign. We had to make Alger likable before we tried to sell the energy company as eco-friendly. It was truly laughable; however, Alger was paying a mint, so we'd delivered a great plan.

I was missing some details about one of the charities Lenard had told me about and pulled out my notes when the folder he'd left fell off the couch, its contents spilling and papers scattering on the floor.

I gathered them neatly to put them back when the top sheet caught my attention. It wasn't charity information; it was an invoice from AmeriMed.

Anesthesia machine, connectors and valves, breathing circuit, artificial resuscitators. What the hell was this? I moved to the next page and it was more medical equipment. Defibrillators, ECG machine, infusion pumps, there were pages of expensive machines. I was so confused at what I was looking at. There weren't only machines but supplies as well. The invoices ranged from a year old to just a few weeks ago. The bills were addressed to an LJ Glass with a PO Box here in Florida. I flipped through the pages again and all the purchase orders were listed as Horizon III.

A quick internet search came up with an old oil platform that Alger owned, but it hadn't been operational for many years. Something wasn't right. I snagged my phone out of my bag and called the one person that I knew would help me.

"Hello?"

"Hey Blake, how are you?"

"Eh. Morning sickness sucks. How's Florida?" she asked.

"Eh. Hot, humid, sandy. I hope I'm not bothering you, but I was hoping you could help me. But before I ask, you can tell me no. I know you're busy at work."

"Sure, what do you need?"

Now that I had her on the phone I was second guessing myself. Why did I even care about some invoices anyway? It wasn't part of my scope of work. It had no bearing on whether or not I could do my job.

"I feel silly bothering you. It's something I found in a file at work. I'm being nosy, that's all. Something felt off, but now that I'm thinking about it I feel bad about wasting your time."

"If something feels off, Reagan, trust your gut. What is it? I'm sure I can help."

"I'm working on a PR campaign, and while I was at the client's office I took a file home on accident. I looked in the file; it's full of invoices with a PO notation - Horizon III..." There was a knock on my door cutting me off. "Hold on; someone's at the door."

"Horizon III? Reagan, what oil company are you working with?" she asked as I looked through the peephole seeing Lenard standing outside my door.

Jesus this guy is a creep. How the hell did he get my home address?

"My boss is at the door," I told her.

"Reagan! What oil company?"

"Alger Energy."

"Do not answer the door."

It was too late. I already unlocked the door and started to open.

"Lenard, what are you doing here?" I asked.

"Hang up the phone." His voice was demanding and much harder than I'd ever heard.

"Don't hang up. Just set the phone down, leave the line open so I can hear."

"Okay. Talk to you later," I said into the phone and lowered it from my ear.

What the hell was going on? Why was Blake freaking out? She sounded almost scared. Why would she care what company I was working with?

Lenard silently stalked toward me, backing me into my apartment, slamming the door behind him.

"It's a shame."

Then my world went dark.

20

My attention had piqued when I heard Blake talking to Reagan on the phone, but I tried to be as nonchalant as I could while I eavesdropped on the conversation. It seemed like chit-chat until Blake's voice got hard and she started to question Reagan about her employer.

An oil company?

It had to be a coincidence.

Blake had the whole team's attention when she told Reagan not to answer her door. She put her cell on speaker, and for the first time in over a month, I felt my heart beat when I heard her voice.

"Lenard, what are you doing here?" she asked.

My heart stopped. She had a man. I couldn't listen to her greeting her boyfriend.

"Hang up the phone." He sounded like a dick; a rude one. I immediately hated him and not because I was jealous of him. The thought that anyone would speak to her in such a harsh tone pissed me off. I'd talk to Jasper about telling Rea to dump his ass if this was how he treated her.

"Don't hang up. Just set the phone down, leave the line open so I can hear," Blake said at the same time she wrote ALGER OIL on a piece of paper and held it up, then pointing to the whiteboard that displayed pictures of the Horizon III.

"Okay. Talk to you later," Reagan said then there was movement and rustling, but she hadn't hung up.

There was silence for a beat then a door slamming before his next words made my blood run cold.

"It's a shame."

The line went dead, and my insides turned to stone.

It had been hours and still no word from Reagan. Her phone was off, and she hadn't gone into the office. Levi was able to hack into her computer and activate her laptop camera. Unfortunately, it didn't tell us much as it was facing the cushions of her couch. The feed was live streaming on one of our large monitors just in case someone came back to her apartment.

Blake had contacted one of her connections to access any CCTV city cameras in the area surrounding her building. It was taking too fucking long. This asshole could've taken her anywhere by now.

"What did she say again?" I asked Blake again.

She didn't complain when she went through the conversation again.

"Invoices?" I asked rhetorically. "What invoices referencing the Horizon III could she have found that bothered her so badly she'd call you about them?"

I knew she didn't have the answer to that, but we were missing something.

Blake's phone rang and after a short conversation she hung up and grabbed her laptop.

She asked Levi to connect her to the big screen. When he did, CCTV footage from a traffic cam came on showing Reagan being walked to an awaiting car at the curb. Lenard Glass had his hand on her bicep, easily directing her into the backseat. He followed, joining her in the backseat and the car sped away.

The next hour was used to isolate and enhance the two-minute video. Facial recognition verified what we knew, the man who'd taken Reagan was indeed, Lenard Glass Jr, CEO of Alger. The driver was still unknown, even though we had a clear image of his face.

"Wait. Let me see the driver again," Blake stopped us before we could change the image.

She rummaged through her desk until she found what she wanted. "Thought so!" she exclaimed and held up a picture. "Same man as the tugboat captain I was following in Texas."

I examined both images, and she was correct. The driver and the tug captain were one in the same.

"Damn, you're good," Levi praised.

"Plate came back to LJG Holdings," Lenox announced.

"Lenard Jr. Glass," I surmised.

"Levi and Blake, run LJG Holdings, see what exactly they *hold* and check out LJ Glass, that's the only alias I can dig up. Jasper, go through the rest of the CCTV footage. Clark, you come with me." Lenox walked me through the hangar and outside. He was leaned against the building watching me pace in front of him.

"Fuck!"

Lenox remained quiet.

"I let her go. What the hell was I thinking? I should've told her. You know what stopped me?"

Lenox didn't answer.

"My damn pride. The last night she looked unaffected she was leaving, happy even. I got pissed because I felt like she was ripping my heart out of my chest and there she was smiling."

He still hadn't said anything.

"I told her that I didn't want a relationship, that I wasn't capable of it. After what Stephanie and Nick did to me I never thought I'd want another woman for more than a few nights. She knew the score. Agreed that we would have some fun then she'd leave. Goddamnit, I fell in love with her. I didn't even try and stop it. I couldn't. That first time in my car, her listening to that shit music acting goofy as hell, blurting out anything and everything that popped into her head – I knew I could love her. She's honest to a fault and calls me on my shit. No one has ever done that. And I let her leave even though I love her. I've been dying a slow, painful death and I still didn't call her and tell her. Now some prick has her, and I may never see her again. All for what? My fucking pride."

Lenox remained watchful, not interrupting my thoughts.

"I'm going to find her and bring her ass home. Here to Georgia where she belongs. If she doesn't feel the same way, I'll wait her out. Hell, if you could talk Lily into marrying your ass and pop out your boys, surely I can do it."

"You straight?" he asked.

"Yeah."

"Great. Good talk." Lenox laughed and held open the door for me.

"How'd it go?" Jasper yelled to Lenox when we entered.

"So much easier than the rest of ours. He didn't even punch me in the face. You both owe me fifty," he answered.

"Fuckers!"

It would've been funny if I hadn't been so worried about Reagan.

After Lenox had freaked out and left Lily, he almost beat the hell out of Jasper when he found out Jasper knew Lily was pregnant with Carter and he still allowed her to leave. During Jasper's meltdown, when the guilt of his first child's death got to be so much he'd bailed on Emily, he came to the hangar and beat the punching bag until his fists were bloodied. Both Lily and I had to talk him down. Then there was Levi. His dumb ass had allowed a misunderstanding to drive a wedge between him and Blake for years. I'd cashed in every favor I was owed by the brass to get Blake transferred to the 707, so the two of them could work out their shit. It worked like a charm, and she hadn't even officially been embedded with the team for two hours before he drug her to the courthouse and married her. After I'd watched my three best friends lose their minds over their women, I still hadn't taken my own advice to them and held on to her when I had her.

The car had been a dead end, it had come back registered to LJG Holdings. There was no sign of it after it pulled away from the curb. We caught a break when Levi and Blake found what tipped Reagan off. Medical invoices. The purchase orders referencing the Horizon III matched up to what she'd told Blake. But other than that piece of information, we'd hit a dead end.

I was running out of time. I had to get home to Nick, it was almost time for Anna to leave. Fuck. At this rate, I was going to be bald by the time the night was over if I kept yanking at my hair. I had to go, but I had to stay too. Maybe I could run home and pick up Nick and bring him back here. He could chill on the couch and play on his tablet. Not the most responsible parental choice, but it was all I had.

"Em's gonna go pick up, Nick. You cool with that?" Jasper asked.

"Damn, you read my mind."

"Figured. Call Anna and tell her. Em will be there in ten minutes. She'll grab the boys a pizza."

I excused myself to make the call and explained the situation to Anna. She was a godsend and told me she'd have Nick pack some PJ's just in case I ran later than expected. And we did. It was after midnight by the time we left the hangar. Most of what we'd found wouldn't help us find Reagan. The only new lead was an LJG Holdings helicopter had put in a flight plan with the FAA flying to South Padre Island, Texas. The flight plan hadn't had a departure date, so we were still blind as far as that was concerned.

After we did more research on South Padre Island and the surrounding area, we found there had been a breach at a pharmaceutical lab, PharmaC. It was unclear what had been taken from the lab, but the feds had been brought in. Blake enlisted the help of her contact again to track down what was manufactured in the facility. It could be a coincidence, but the medical connection was too much to ignore.

I tried Reagan's cell phone again on the drive to Jasper's and left her another message. If I was honest with myself, I'd only called so I could hear her voice on her message. She sounded so happy and carefree.

Full of life.

I was going to kill Lenard Glass when I got my hands on him. The method was dependent on the condition we found Reagan in. And we would find her. If she was unharmed, I'd take pity on him and make it quick, but if one strand of her pretty blonde hair was harmed, I'd disembowel him.

The tap on my window scared the shit out of me. I hadn't realized I'd pulled into Jasper's driveway. As a matter of fact, I didn't remember the drive over.

I stepped out of the Jeep and Jasper looked about as concerned as I did.

"We'll find her," I assured him.

"Goddamn right we will."

My lips almost twitched at the violence in his tone. None of us backed down from an enemy, but when you make it personal and take what belongs to us, hellfire will rain down.

"She's strong, brother. She'll hold on until we can get there."

"How do you know?" he asked.

"Because she's mine and there isn't another option. Reagan is tough; she'll give that dick a run for his money."

"Glad to hear it. It's about time you admit it."

"Yeah, well I knew before she left. I should've

said something then. I won't make that mistake again.
I hope you don't have a problem with it, because the
minute we get her back, she's in my house, with my
ring on her finger, and I'm gonna make that shit legal
as soon as I can. It would make things a hell of a lot
easier if you had my back."

"I knew the day I watched you, watching her in
the backyard. I've known you a long time, and I'd
never seen you so enraptured with a woman. I'll
take your back. She won't fight it; I know she
loves you."

"I hope to hell she does because I'm in misery
without her."

I collected Nick, thanked Emily for taking care
of my nephew, and drove us home. This time I'd paid
a bit more attention driving because Nick was in the
car, but not much. I was getting Nick settled in his
room when he stopped me.

"How's Reagan?" he asked.

Shit, he'd overheard something.

"What'd you hear?" I asked, sitting on his bed.

"I wasn't trying to snoop," he defended himself.

"Bud, I didn't think you were. I was gonna tell
you when I knew more."

"Emily said that no one has heard from her and it
didn't look good."

My teeth ground together until I might've chipped a tooth.

"We're going to find her. I don't have a lot of information to tell you other than she found out something about her boss he didn't want her to know. The last time she was seen, the man was pushing her into a car."

"Will she come back home?"

"What do you mean?"

"Here. Will she come home when you find her?"

We'd talked about Reagan since she'd left, and I knew he liked her, but we'd never hid that she was only in Georgia visiting.

"Would you be okay if she came here to live with us?"

"It's your hou..."

I cut him off. "Wrong answer, Nicholas. This is your home. Our home. We discuss major decisions that will affect both of us before they're made. We're a team. Do you want her here?"

"Yes. I miss her. But I didn't want to say anything to you because I knew you were missing her too and it might hurt your feelings if I asked about her."

Damn the boy was perceptive and thoughtful. Both great qualities. I hated that he'd learned those traits because he'd had a drunk of a mother that he'd had to take care of. Stephanie was another issue we had to discuss. Once the occupants of the car she ran off the road died, she'd taken a plea deal. Two life sentences - the plea came in when the DA left a possibility of parole on the table. Not that I was worried about her being let out of prison anytime soon. Nick needed to know what was going on with her, and permanent custody needed to be discussed. But now was not the time.

"I appreciate your concern, but in the future, please don't hide your feelings from me. Even if you think they'll hurt my feelings. I want you to be able to tell me anything. And yes, I miss her very much. I wish I would've told her how much I loved her before she left. However, I plan on rectifying that immediately and bring her home."

We talked a bit more about his day and the work he'd done with Anna until he started yawning. We both needed some sleep. I had a hunch that tomorrow was going to be a long day.

Hold tight baby; I'm coming for you.

21

"I know you're awake. No sense pretending."

My head hurt, even trying to pull a coherent thought to the forefront made the pounding intensify. I cracked one eye open, then the other. A fuzzy image of a man was swimming in front of me, making me dizzy. I closed my eyes and willed myself to remember. Where the hell was I? The pain was too intense for me to be scared. I was more pissed than anything. I didn't like the way I felt.

"Lenard?" I managed.

"You know it didn't have to be this way. It's all your fault, you nosy bitch."

What the hell was he talking about? Be what way? Nosy? I scanned my memories and tried to make heads or tails of what he was saying.

I was at his office going over donations I could use in my press release to make Alger look like a responsible environmental consequence company, which was not only absurd but basically impossible. I went home, wrote my copy, reviewed what I wrote, and...it was right there on the fringe of my memory. I did something else. Why did my head hurt? Maybe I didn't go home, and something happened to me at the office; that's why Lenard is here.

"Where am I?"

"It doesn't matter," he answered.

Why the hell was he mad at me? And what the freak did he mean it didn't matter?

"It does, Lenard. Where. Am. I?"

Shit, even that small amount of ire made me want to vomit. I tried to lift my hands to rub the pain on my temples, but my hands wouldn't move. I struggled to move them to no avail.

"Stop moving. You'll pull out your IV," he scolded.

The memory I needed was dancing in the corner of my mind. It was right there. The missing piece I needed.

"They're not ready for you. Go back to sleep."

No! I didn't want to sleep. I wanted to remember.

Clark! I needed Clark.

Warmth rushed through my veins and peace washed over my body. I no longer cared where I was or why. The pain was gone, and I was slipping back into the darkness.

Sweet oblivion.

22

"It's been too fucking long."

I'd lost my patience about twenty-four hours ago. Reagan had been gone twenty-five hours. That was a long fucking time in the hands of a madman. The hell of it was we were all pretty sure we knew where she was. The helicopter made the trip to Texas and the tugboat that Blake had been watching made a trip out to the Horizon III and was currently sitting docked to the rig.

Our problem was we didn't have clearance to board the platform. We were currently being choked by red tape. The Commander was trying his best to help, but his hands were tied. He'd reviewed our intel and agreed something illegal was going on out in the middle of The Gulf, but his hands were tied, too. He also agreed that Reagan was more than likely being held on the platform. But other than that, we were dead in the water. The Commander couldn't sanction a rescue mission using his top-secret black ops team. The higher-ups would not be happy with the misuse.

"Tell me again, what was taken from the Pharma lab," the Commander asked, looking at the intel report on PharmaC.

Blake explained that most of the drugs that were taken were anti-rejection meds; Immunosuppressive, anti-proliferative, calcineurin inhibitor, as well as pain management narcotics.

"What else does the lab manufacture or store on premises?" he asked, flipping through the pages.

Blake didn't answer right away; she was working through the question the Commander had asked. After a few moments of contemplation, she ignored the Commander's inquiry; instead, she started down a different path of investigation.

"Levi pull up the Lethal Unitary Chemical Agents and Munitions list from the Chemical Weapons Convention. Lenox, check the CWC schedule. There are three schedules that outline toxic chemicals and their use. We want any material on Schedule I or II. Those chemicals have few non-legitimate uses. Clark check those feeds again, make sure no one has left the platform. While you're doing that, go back through the invoices and see if you can find a hypothermic machine."

"Best goddamn decision I ever made. Brilliant," the Commander said.

Blake was on to something, and I knew better than to question her or ask for clarification. The Commander was spot on; she was brilliant. The tug was still tied to the floating dock under the platform. It wasn't a clear image, but every once in a while, I caught sight of the stern bobbing up and down.

"We got something," Levi announced. "3-Quinu-clidinyl benzilate," he said, butchering the pronunciation. "Better known as QBN. It's listed in the Army's database as an incapacitating agent, code 2277."

"Other applications?" Blake asked.

"It was invented as an anti-spasmodic, researched for use in ulcers..." Lenox continued to scan the document reading the specifics as he went. "In the early sixties, the Army started trials using it as a chemical warfare agent, known as BUZZ. Later known as Agent 15 by NATO and the CIA." He scrolled through more information before concluding. "No. QBN is an anticholinergic agent that affects both the peripheral and central nervous systems and is listed as a WMD by NATO."

"Was any taken during the break-in at PhamaC?" the Commander asked.

The team remained quiet, trying to figure out how to phrase the answer to the Commander's question. An affirmative would give us clearance to board the Horizon III but most likely end in an Article-32 investigation. If the answer was negative, we were fucked. The mission wouldn't be approved, and Reagan would be left out in The Gulf to rot, which would leave me no choice but to disobey a direct order and go get her myself.

After weighing my options, I wasn't going to allow the team to lie. I would go in alone, ensuring the rest of the team stayed in the clear.

"There is no way to answer with one-hundred percent certainty. It seems that the laboratory's hard drives have been scrubbed. There is no way to confirm the inventory prior to the breach, and now I fear it could take days, weeks even, to sift through the paper copies and hand count each specimen they have on premises. At this point the only response I feel comfortable giving you is my professional opinion and best guess," Blake told the Commander.

"And your professional opinion is?" he asked.

"The United States does not have the option to wait while a proper investigation is completed when a manufacturing facility has been breached. QBN is classified as a weapon of mass destruction; releasing it would be catastrophic."

The Commander weighed her statement carefully before walking to the door. "Wheels up in thirty minutes. Your op is approved. Be safe." He opened the door before turning to Blake. "Your ass is staying here, young lady. Mission logistics only."

"Yes, sir," Blake easily agreed.

Not that any of us were going to allow her to accompany us on an op while she was pregnant anyway. I was just happy the Commander had given her a direct order; she wouldn't give him any lip.

Almost there sweetheart. Hold on.

Twenty-minutes later gear had been collected from the cage, and we were ready to roll. I'd called to check in with Nicholas and explained what was going on and that I would not be home tonight. When he found out he'd be staying with Emily and Jasper, his disappointment faded quickly. He loved spending time at their house. The taco truck on base had finally caught up with Jasper, and he was home with food poisoning. I felt bad for him, but I was thankful he'd be home to watch over Nick.

"Wait." Blake stopped us as we headed for the door. "Did you find a hypothermic machine?"

Shit. I'd forgotten to tell her what I'd found. "Yes. There was one listed. What are you thinking?"

"I knew it. KPS-1 and SPS-1 were both taken from the lab as well. Both of those drugs are for flushing and cold storage of organs. Combine that with the anti-rejection drugs and medical equipment onboard; I think they're harvesting organs. They might also be performing the transplant on the platform as well."

"The fuck?" Lenox groused.

"Black market organs are a huge enterprise. I've seen it all over the world. The potential for profit is astronomical. There is always someone in need of a heart or liver."

My stomach was rejecting the images of Reagan being held prisoner and her organs being cut from her body. The saliva pooled too swift for me to swallow, and I grabbed a trashcan and emptied the contents of my stomach. Spitting the last of my lunch into the basket, I left the hangar, trashcan in hand to get rid of the evidence of my failure. Goddamn, we were too late. Lenard had her too long. Fuck. I tossed the trashcan and slammed the lid of the dumper shut, the foul smell of the large metal container making me want to throw up again. Lenard Glass was a dead man. I was going to gut him and lay his organs on the deck of the platform before I tossed his carcass overboard.

"She's strong," Lenox said.

"She'll hold on until we get there," Levi added.

"You need to hold your shit together. She's going to need you. I'm running point. Levi will be my second. Your only job is to get to Reagan; we'll clear your way," Lenox added.

"You know we're right. If she's hurt, all your attention needs to be focused on her," Levi said. "It's go time. We'll have sights on your woman within the hour."

Please God, Rea, hold on. We can deal with anything, as long as you're breathing.

23

Why was I so tired? I was warm and comfy, but I wanted to move. Nothing worked; my limbs were too heavy, even trying to lift my pinky was exhausting. I needed to get up. I needed to pee, or at least I thought I did. Maybe I didn't. Maybe I was dreaming, and all I had to do was wake up.

Open your eyes, Reagan.

I couldn't. They weren't obeying; nothing was.

I was so tired.

"Is she ready?"

Ready? Where was I going? I tried to ask, but no sound would come out.

"Yes."

"And can she hear and feel?"

"Yes. The patient is in an altered state. She is

basically paralyzed; she can hear and will feel the tugging and pulling. The majority of the pain will be dulled with the paralysis."

"Outstanding. What are you taking first?"

"Kidney and a partial liver."

"Is the recipient prepped?"

"For the liver, yes. The kidney will be airlifted out."

This was a shit dream. Why was I dreaming about kidneys and not Clark? Not that I'd slept all that well since I'd left Georgia, but when I finally did drift off it was always into a fantasy world where Clark and I lived together. No stupid agreement between us, nothing holding us back from being together. I was free to love him any way I wanted. And he loved me too. It was double-edged because when I awoke from the fictitious place where all my fantasies and desires came to life, I was crushed when reality seeped in and I remembered that Clark wasn't mine and he never would be.

I wanted to fall into a Clark-fueled dream, not this doctor drama inspired shit. This dream sucked. I tried to reach for the TV remote to turn off whatever medical show I'd fallen asleep watching, but I was too exhausted.

"You ready, Reagan? This may hurt a bit."

24

We'd gone over the plan and the backup plan no less than five times on our way out to the platform. The original plan of a high-altitude drop was nixed due to wind. We couldn't safely parachute in with wind gusts what they were. Fast roping in was an option, but without cover and intel on who was on the rig, we decided against that.

We'd swim in. Piece of cake. All three of us were comfortable in the water, and we could come in soft and unannounced.

"Bravo one. Update."

Blake's smooth voice came to life over my earpiece.

"INFIL boat landing. Moving topside now," Lenox answered.

The comms went silent, and Levi gave the all-clear before we moved to an upper deck. The metal grates under my boots made moving quietly damn near impossible as we surveyed the area. With the deck recon'd and empty, we moved to the next level. The second deck was the same - deserted. There was a sinking feeling in my gut. What if we were wrong and she wasn't here? The third deck was where the drone had captured images of the supplies being dropped.

"Bravo one I see movement above you. One tango," Blake informed us.

"Armed?" Lenox returned.

"Unknown. Came from the west. Blueprint shows the structure as the galley and dining facilities. Attached to the north is crew quarters. The rig hot racks, but without pulling up the berthing diagrams to be a hundred percent, I'd guess you have seventy-five bunks, at least."

More than enough space to set up a black-market hospital in the middle of The Gulf.

"Copy, Bravo two. We're heading that way now."

Lenox pointed to the camera on his vest, reminding me we were being watched, and listened to; his way of telling me not to go rogue and paint this floating house of horrors red with Lenard's blood.

I couldn't make any promises, especially if Reagan was injured.

Lenox wasted no time popping out from behind a container box and choking out the pacing man. He was easily subdued and zip tied to the railing; a pat-down bared no weapons and he was left there. It was eerily quiet on the deck with only the sound of the ocean pounding into the pylons below.

Levi nodded when he was in position to cover Lenox. He slipped past the metal door that had been left open and Levi followed, leaving me to bring up the rear.

The first thing that assaulted me was the smell. A mixture of coppery blood, body decomp, and cleaning solvents; the last obviously not doing a very good job masking the stench. We moved farther into what used to be the dining hall, and the faint sounds of beeping could be heard along with muffled voices. The smell alone was enough to make us quicken our step, but the sudden blood-curdling scream had us triple timing it toward the sound.

"On your knees," Levi yelled, giving up the pretense of stealth.

The sight before me had me thanking all things

holy I had already lost my cookies back at Post because if not, I would've now. A man in scrubs was elbows deep in someone's chest, blood spilling over the paper drape covering their lower body. The identity and gender were unknown.

Fuck.

"Move the fuck away," Lenox demanded.

The man didn't move but did answer. "I am holding his heart in my hand. If I move now, he will die."

His.

The relief that rushed through my body was dizzying. Thank God, not Reagan.

"Bravo one. Two unfriendlies in three...two... now."

Levi and I turned in unison as two men ran into the room, unable to get more than two steps in before we got our shots off, neutralizing the threat.

"Close him up," Lenox told the man, moving to the operating table. "Male, Latino, late teens, early twenties."

I hadn't realized how much I needed the confirmation it wasn't Reagan strapped to the table until Lenox verified.

"Bravo two, we need a great white here, like yesterday. Too many to transport," Levi called in.

I ducked into the room Levi had entered, wondering why he'd call in for the Navy's hospital ship and I was horrified. At first glance, there looked to be at least fifty gurneys filling the space.

"Bravo one, ETA on that is going to be awhile. Closest one is the Comfort and she's off the Panhandle."

"Berthing area one has fifty patients. Hold tight for area two."

"MediVac is on standby for your critical. You are all clear on the outer decks."

Lenox was still barking orders at the doctor in the room.

"Team leader, I'm breaking off. Number two will stay behind," I told Lenox, then tucked my mic so I wouldn't be heard before I turned to Levi. "I'm going to find Reagan."

"I don't think that's a good idea. Once the doc is secure, I'll go with you."

"It could be too late by then. Cover Lenox."

I didn't wait before I took off passing patients - who the fuck was I kidding – they weren't patients. They were prisoners who'd had their organs stolen from them. If the scream from the man whose heart was being removed from his chest was any indication, they were alive when it was being done.

The next compartment was the same, only twenty beds were in here. I called it into Blake so she could keep a running tally of the enormity of what we were dealing with.

I slowed my pace when I heard the muffled voice of a man.

"Yes, sir, they are almost a perfect match. Hazel. Yes. More green than brown. They can be airborne within an hour. Yes. I assure you the donor is very healthy; she has no medical conditions."

The queasiness I'd felt all day subsided, and with great clarity my training kicked in. Lenard was on the other side of the privacy screen negotiating the removal and selling of Reagan's beautiful eyes. Pretty hazel eyes that I had looked into a hundred times, eyes that I loved.

The urge to take my time and torture this man fled. All I wanted was to hold Reagan and get her home. Nick and I could love her back to health.

"Perfect. Have your people wait in Florida. The donor is prepped and ready to go."

Target.

Not Reagan.

I had to slow my heart rate and think of her as the target. She deserved nothing less than my all. I had saved hundreds of men in combat. I've gone up against the worst men this world had to offer. This was the most important mission of my life; I wouldn't fuck it up.

I pulled my knife out of the sheath at my hip and secured my HK45 to the webbing on the front of my tactical vest. Just because I wasn't going to take the time to torture him didn't mean I was going to show him mercy. A bullet was too quick, too painless.

I waited behind the white curtain a beat waiting for Lenard to walk out from behind the screen. As soon as he did, I caught him around the neck in a chokehold, pulling his back to my front. I held him there. His struggles were futile, the more he moved, the tighter my forearm pressed against the side of his throat, cutting off the blood flow to his brain. Lenard's body started to go limp, and I loosened my grip on his neck. I wanted him awake when I took his life.

"You fucked with the wrong woman," I growled, pushing the tip of my Kabar into the side of his neck, waiting until I felt his warm blood coat my hand before moving my blade. "How about we arrange for the removal of your organs?" I sliced through his flesh like it was nothing more than softened butter. I was more than halfway across his throat when the gurgling of oxygen leaving his body, mixed with the blood now freely flowing, slowed to a rattle. "Rot in hell, fucker." I shoved my blade deep and his body slouched, lifeless in my arms.

A good man would tell you he took no pleasure ending a life. It was simply done in protection of others. I, however, am not a good man. I'd purposefully removed my gloves before I slit his throat. I wanted to feel his life's blood drain from his body, knowing it was my hand that had stolen it, as he had stolen so many other's lives. I wouldn't say I took pleasure spilling his blood, but I did feel satisfaction.

Without giving any more thought to Lenard Glass, I dropped him to the floor like the trash he was and cleaned my hands on the legs of my pants. After a short mental pep talk I pushed aside the privacy curtain, and there she was.

"Eye on the prize," I called in.

"SITREP," Blake's answering question was full of relief.

"Compartment left of the second berthing. Breathing, vitals look strong." I pushed down the white sheet that covered her and was tucked under her armpits.

Fuck.

Fuck.

Fuck.

"Bravo one?" Blake called.

I bent at the middle, bracing my hands on my knees to catch my breath.

"Bravo one." She repeated.

Reagan was completely nude, an angry puckered scar on her left side. Black sutures tied her skin together. They looked like she'd been stitched by a preschooler, obviously uncaring of the scar it would leave. Not that cosmetics mattered to these sick fucks. I bet the only reason she was sewn up was to keep her alive long enough to harvest the next body part they wanted.

"Clark!" Levi's voice cut through my musings.

"Alive."

That was all I could manage.

Breathing.

All I needed was her breathing.

That was the mantra I repeated over the next excruciating forty-eight hours, then days that followed.

I could love her through anything.

25

"I'm gonna strangle him," I told Nick and winked.

"Cut him some slack; he thought you were going to die."

Damn, I loved this kid. Him and I, we were two peas in a pod. He had no filter either. He didn't think about what he was saying before he blurted it out. I loved it.

"I'm fine. I think I can get up and get my own ice cream."

"Not according to him. And what do you care if Nolan gets you a bowl of ice cream?"

Little shit. He was right. I didn't care. As a matter of fact, I liked Clark taking care of me. It had been a month since he saved me from the Rig Reaper. The guys hated when I joked about my time in the middle of The Gulf on the gigantic metallic island of madness, but if I didn't tease about it, I'd go crazy. So, I lost a kidney and part of my liver. That was still better than what most of the others had lost.

There were one hundred and forty of us on the rig that day. One hundred of us made it off the platform alive. The worst of us had been airlifted out; the rest waited for the USS Comfort, a huge floating hospital the Navy used for humanitarian efforts and relief.

When I woke up in the hospital, I was in Georgia; everyone was there, even Clark's Commander. The over-protective, Neanderthal behavior started the moment I'd opened my eyes. When my incision became infected, and I had to remain in the hospital another week, I thought Clark was going to have a come apart. He'd flat out refused to talk to me about what happened. Bits and pieces of Lenard taking me from my apartment had come back, but I don't remember anything about my time on the platform. My doctor assured me it was normal with the number of drugs I'd been given, and I more than likely would never be able to recall the details. I was okay with that. I didn't want to know. I wasn't in denial. I recognized that I'd been kidnapped, held against my will, drugged, and I was now missing a kidney because one was stolen from me. But I was alive. One thing I can remember when I was waking up in the hospital is Clark repeating *as long as you're breathing baby, I'll love you through anything.* I believed that. I wasn't going to let what happened break me.

Clark?

I was working on him. When I was discharged from the hospital, I'd found that my apartment in Florida had been packed up – by my mother. Thankfully I was on a plethora of pain meds, hooked up to monitors, and had more wires and leads than a marionette, or I would've run screaming for the hills. No twenty-something woman wants her mother to pack her apartment – trust and believe that. I'm sure my mom got an eyeful when she packed the contents of my nightstand drawer. Sheesh. I may never look at my mother again. So, there I was, moved into Clark's house before I'd even woken up. I didn't argue or complain. I never wanted to step foot back into that apartment, but more importantly, I was getting what I wanted – a chance to be with Clark.

"If I were you? I'd totally milk it. He's so in love with you, he'd do anything you wanted," Nick said conspiratorially.

"No, he wouldn't." I laughed, trying to pretend

Nick's observation that Clark loved me didn't make me want to jump for joy. Not that I would, because Clark would have a heart attack and die if I so much as eased off the couch, let alone jump.

"Sure, he does." Nick gave me a look that conveyed exactly what he wanted it to – duh.

"Does what?" Clark asked, carrying my ice cream back to the couch.

"Love Reagan," Nick blurted.

My death ray must've been rusty because he didn't immediately burst into flames for embarrassing me.

Clark chuckled and shook his head.

"Christ. There's two of you. Let it all hang out – anytime, anywhere." Clark handed me the bowl and sat down next to me, gathered me close, and kissed the top of my head. "Yes, Nick, I love Reagan. Though I have to say, I haven't told her yet. So maybe we can be cool and wait until I have a minute alone with her and I can tell her."

"Ummm...." Nick stuttered.

"Kidding bud."

Wait!

Kidding about what? That he loved me or that he was teasing Nick? What was I supposed to do now? I had to know.

Clark didn't make me wait long before he kissed my temple, this time whispering, "Love you, Rea."

"I love you, too."

He loved me.

Best day ever!

I'd totally give up a kidney again if it meant Clark would rescue me and tell me he loved me.

26

"Wait. What?" That was Reagan's response.

Jasper told me a long time ago I had no tact. At the time I thought he was wrong. However, judging by Rea's response, I'm thinking Jasper may've been correct in his assessment.

"I want you to move in."

Simple. Straightforward. To the point. I didn't see the issue.

"Um, Clark, I'm going to need more information than that."

I was missing something, or she was because my statement was self-explanatory.

"Are you having issues with the English language, woman?"

If she were any other woman, I'd think she was

fishing, but Reagan was a straight shooter. She didn't play games, and neither was I, but I couldn't find the disconnect.

She rolled her eyes and threw a pillow at me.

"Stop. You might pull a stitch," I scolded.

"Enough." Reagan stopped smiling. "The doctor gave me the all clear. I'm healthy."

I assure you the donor is very healthy; she has no medical conditions.

"Where'd you go?" she asked.

"Nowhere. Sorry. I want you to move in permanently. Not just *stay* here until you recover."

Reagan remained quiet for a moment, and I didn't like how long it was taking her to answer.

"What happened on the platform?"

Death. Fear. Horror.

"I've already told you. Nothing worth talking about."

"You dream about it." Shit. I was hoping I hadn't woken her when I had dreams about her being strapped to the bed with the doctor elbow deep in her chest cavity yanking her heart out while she screamed. "It's not like the first night-mare I walked in on. You whimper and beg me not to die. Other times you apologize for letting me die."

I was horrified I'd talked in my sleep and she heard.

Christ.

"I'll move in with you if you talk to me. It's not good to keep everything locked up."

"Baby. I have more shit locked away than a bank vault."

She was looking at me expectantly. I couldn't believe she was blackmailing me into talking about something I absolutely did not want to speak about.

"Why do you want to know? There are some things you're better off not remembering. Be happy either the anesthesia those hacks gave you kept you from knowing what was going on, or your brain is protecting you and blocking it out."

"Was it that bad?" she asked.

Was she fucking crazy?

"Worse than you can imagine!"

"You're not in the regular Army, are you?"

Whoa. Subject change, a welcomed one. We needed to have this conversation anyway. Before she committed to a relationship with me, she needed the facts.

"No. Remember when we talked about Combat Applications Group?"

"Yeah. Special Forces team, right? A CAG team saved you when you were captured."

"Yes. What I do for the Army isn't something I talk about. None of us do. It's not because we're secretive for shits and grins. We literally can't. The 707 is attached to the 1st Special Forces Operational Detachment." I waited for some sort of understanding to dawn, but it didn't. "This is going to be painful."

"What is?"

"Explaining my team this way; have you heard of Delta Force?" I almost rolled my eyes saying that. No operator I knew would call themselves Delta. We were special operators, SFOD, ACE, Task Force Green - the Army had many names for us, the one we avoided the most was Delta. That was what Hollywood and video games liked to use. It was sensationalized as if the word Delta didn't translate into death – elite deadly warfighters. To them, it was great for headlines. Delta Force and Navy SEALs, the media loved to exploit war.

"Of course. Ohhh...wait...are you?"

"I've never had to explain what I am and you not having an understanding of the military is making this difficult. The 707 is a twenty-man unit - four men, five teams. Officially, the 707 is a research and development regiment. Unofficially, we're a black ops team. We get sent in when the government wants complete deniability. Jasper and Lenox were pulled from Ranger school when they showed outstanding potential. Levi and I were both on an SFOD team when we were pulled to join the 707."

"That sounds dangerous, Clark."

"It is. I won't lie to you. Each time I leave on an op, there's a chance I won't come home." Reagan's face paled, and I hurried to finish. "But that's true for most jobs in the military. When units deploy, they aren't going on vacation; they're going into a war zone."

"What happened when you found me?"

The woman was giving me whiplash. I guess she was done with job descriptions and was moving on to mental anguish.

"The first room we entered was...disturbing." Was I really doing this - debriefing sweet, innocent Reagan. I didn't need to close my eyes to recall the details. They were always at the forefront of my memory. "One male doctor. Two female nurses. The doctor was performing cardiac surgery to remove a man's heart – to sell it."

Reagan had gone pale again, and I was rethinking telling her more.

"Go on. Where was I?"

"I found you in one of the berthing compartments that had been converted into a makeshift recovery ward. There were two rooms that held patients in various stages of... I don't know what to call it... recovery... waiting to have more of their organs, joints, and bones taken from their bodies to sell. You were in a room by yourself."

She shifted and slid down from leaning against the headboard to rest her head on my chest. Somehow telling her the details when she wasn't looking at me with her pretty eyes -eyes that were almost stolen from her – made it slightly easier.

Fuck!

"Go on, Nolan," she whispered, running her fingers back and forth across my chest.

On an exhale, I went on. "Lenard was with you. He was on the phone negotiating." When I didn't say anything more, she prompted me to continue. "He had a buyer that was interested in purchasing your eyes." Reagan sucked in a breath, and I seriously considered putting a stop to this madness. She didn't need to know this shit. It was jacked.

"I need to know."

"He told the buyer that your eyes were perfect, you were healthy, and prepped for surgery. He promised your eyes would be airborne within an hour."

"That didn't happen," she whispered.

"No, baby, it didn't."

"You saved me."

"No, I didn't." I didn't get there soon enough, or she'd still have both kidneys.

"You did. Wanna know how I know?" she asked, and flattened her hand and placed it over my heart.

"How?" I asked.

"Because I can see." She giggled. "Too soon?" She continued to laugh.

"Ya think?" I snapped.

"Listen. I'm alive. You saved my life and, as a bonus, you saved a hundred other people on the rig as well. Not to mention you and the team helped shut down Larry's fucked up organization. That's a win. That's how we're thinking about this."

The FBI had a field day sifting through LJ Glass Holdings. Other government agencies had to be called in as well as law enforcement in three other countries. Luckily, the Horizon III was the only make-shift hospital. As far as I knew, they were still dismantling the network he'd created.

"You're missing a fucking kidney, Reagan, and part of your liver."

"Yeah, Clark," she sassed. "I know. Lucky for me I had two. One plus a spare. You know that people live with one kidney all the time. My liver has already started to regenerate. I'm healthy."

"Stop saying you're healthy. That's what that fucker said. Very healthy, no medical conditions. Fuck, Rea. That's all I can hear. Lenard talking about you like you weren't a person. He wanted to sell your goddamn eyes. Do you understand? I didn't know if you were dead or alive; if they'd already butchered you. I was so afraid I was going to fail, and you were going to die. It gutted me that he wanted to take your beautiful eyes from me. I died a thousand deaths thinking I'd never get a chance to look into them again. Fuck. When you look at me... it's...everything."

Reagan sat up, and before I could stop her she was sitting astride me, both her hands on my face, forcing me to meet her gaze.

"Look at me, Nolan. Really look at me. You saved me. You got there. See?" I finally met her stare, and relief didn't begin to cover what I felt looking into her eyes. "I love you, Nolan. You said you could love me through anything. And you did. You are. Right back atcha'. Don't hide from me."

"You heard that?"

"I did. God knows you told me enough. *As long as you're breathing, baby*. I heard you, Nolan. You need to stop worrying so much. You're gonna drive yourself crazy. I think you have grey hair now and everything. I'm worried that your gonna need to trim your nose hair soon, and maybe even need those little blue pills, which will be a shame because it's been ... it's been like, forever, since I've gotten laid."

"I love you so fucking much."

Damn, it felt good to laugh, and once it started, I couldn't stop it. The hilarity died down, and I held her stare. Beautiful hazel orbs, more green than brown, shone brightly. She was here and breathing. That was a win.

"You straight?" she asked.

"You movin' in?" I returned.

"Yes."

"Then, yes."

"You think I can get some?" She winked and wiggled her eyebrows.

"Nope."

"Party pooper," she whined and ground down on my unused throbbing cock.

"If you're a good girl and lie still, I'll take care of you."

"Yippy!"

Beauty comes in many different packages. All shapes and sizes. Reagan's beauty didn't come from the outside - it was deep within her. A bright light, a beacon calling me home. I was there, free of my past. And freedom never tasted sweeter.

EPILOGUE

Seven years later

Nolan Clark rolled over and kissed his wife before he tagged his cell off the nightstand and quietly slipped out of their bedroom. She'd been up all night with Jackson, their five-year-old, who had brought home whatever germ was floating around his kindergarten class. Jasper was pissed his daughter had come down with the bug as well, as if it was Clark's fault Jasper's second-born daughter chased Jack around until she could pin him down and kiss him.

Jasper and Emily were in trouble with that one. She was a firecracker with her father's personality and her mother's jet-black hair and crystal blue eyes. His worst nightmare had come to fruition much to the amusement of the women. Four daughters, all two years apart, except for his last two. Twins. When Emily announced she was pregnant with Hadley and Adalynn, the women had jumped for joy, and big bad Jasper Walker had fallen on his ass.

"Hi Daddy," Jackson called out to his father from his perch at the kitchen counter, where he was spreading copious amounts of grape jelly on his toast.

"You think you're gonna eat any bread with the sugar?" Clark gently scolded.

He'd lost the battle on sugary treats in the house long ago, but he still commented on it whenever he could. His boys were lucky to have Reagan for a variety of reasons - grape jelly and chips were just two of those reasons. If it'd been up to him, the kids would eat veggies every day, something that Reagan had explained to him would be something akin to torture. He gave in. Nolan Clark gave in a lot. It didn't take a lot to remind him how short life was. All he had to do was look into his wife's beautiful eyes. It had been almost seven years since Reagan had been taken and he'd almost lost the love of his life. Clark had never again wasted an opportunity to tell her how much he loved her. He was a smart man; he knew Rea was one-in-a-million.

"When will Nick be awake? I want to give him

his graduation present before we get ready to go to the school," Jackson said, completely ignoring his father's comment.

"Soon. How are you feeling?"

"My tummy doesn't hurt anymore."

Clark went about his morning making coffee and answering emails, enjoying the peace before the excitement of the day descended on his house. Reagan had planned a huge graduation party for Nick. He'd be leaving for college soon to start football practice before the rest of the students checked in. Clark didn't know how he felt about that. He'd only had Nick for seven years. He'd missed the first eleven; something that Reagan had helped him forgive Stephanie for. They'd never heard from Stephanie again. Not when permanent custody was awarded, and not when Clark and Reagan had taken it a step further and officially adopted Nicholas. For once in her life, Stephanie Clark had done the right thing. She'd given Nicholas the life he deserved.

"Umm. You smell good." Reagan came to a stop behind her husband and buried her face in Clark's neck.

Clark chuckled at his wife. He loved whenever she entered a room, even if her boys were close by, she always came to Clark first. Always. After she'd planted a kiss on his lips, then she turned to the boys sitting on the couch where Nick was opening Jack's present, and greeted them like she hadn't seen them in years instead of hours. That was something else Rea did – she loved openly. The boys knew she loved them - she told them often and showed them frequently.

Nolan Clark was one lucky son of a bitch, and he knew it.

FOUR YEARS AFTER THAT...

"We're gonna be late. Jackson, hurry up." Reagan looked at her son who was watching TV. What he wasn't doing was tying his shoes.

"Bud, listen to your mother," Clark backed her up.

"One more minute. The arson inspector is getting ready to explain which accelerants were used. Did you know that regular alcohol like vodka is flammable?" Jackson asked, turning his attention back to the TV.

Clark would've been worried they had a firebug on their hands if Jackson wasn't more interested in how to put a fire out, than watching it burn. His

fascination started four years ago when his kindergarten class took a field trip to the fire station. Clark
and Reagan thought it was a phase, but it had yet to
wane. Jackson's thirst for knowledge had only grown
over the years.

"Jackson. You have this documentary at home.
You've watched it a hundred times. Everyone is
waiting for us downstairs," Reagan tried again to get
her son to obey. "Quinn's here," she reminded
Jackson.

That did it. Jackson jumped up, turned off the
TV, and slipped on his shoes in record time. Quinn
Walker was a few months younger than Jackson and
his best friend. The two of them were inseparable.
Thick as thieves, and when you added her sister,
Jasper's first-born daughter, Delaney, into the equa-
tion the group, knew they were in trouble. Delaney
was two years older than her sister and just over a
year older than Jackson. The three of them were
trouble.

Clark looked around at his family. They had
grown in numbers over the years.

It started with four.

Four men, a brotherhood.

They'd shared a bond that was so unbreakable,
when they'd found their other halves they too were

embedded into the fold. Four had turned into eight. Then the children came, completing their tribe of eighteen.

They now took up two rows as they settled in all together. Just as they did when Nick had graduated high school, again they were gathered together four years later when Nick had graduated college.

Now they'd made the trip to Virginia to watch Nicholas Clark accept his latest achievement.

"Fidelity. Bravery. Integrity. For the last twenty weeks, every man and woman seated in the front have lived, breathed, and honored those words. They mean something slightly different for each new Agent Trainee, but the core remains steadfast..."

Reagan squeezed Clark's hand, bringing his attention from the Director addressing the audience to her.

"He did it," she whispered.

"There was never a doubt," he told her.

"No, there wasn't. You did that. Taught him about sacrifice and service."

"We all did," Clark corrected.

The new Agent trainees stood, raised their right hands, and took a sacred oath to protect the Constitution before they walked across the stage to receive their credentials and a shiny gold badge. When Nick stopped to take his from the Director, he turned and found his family in the crowd. They were all there, smiling and clapping. He stopped to enjoy this moment - looking at each of them – all seventeen. Nick didn't care that he was holding up the line. His four uncles deserved this day as much as he did. They'd taught him to be a man. His four aunts had taught him how to love – both giving and receiving it. Those four women had taken a broken boy and loved him until he'd known no different.

Yeah. This day belonged to all of them.

His family.

After the ceremony was over Nick's cousins were passing around his shield, touching it and reading his credentials, when the Director stopped to speak with them.

"Special Agent Clark. Congratulations and welcome to the FBI. We are pleased to have such a fine man join our ranks."

"Thank you, sir."

Nick was filled with pride hearing his newly earned title.

"Introduce me to the rest of your family. I don't believe I've met them all," the Director requested.

"Sir, this is my Uncle Nolan and Aunt Reagan Clark, my brother, Jackson, my Uncle Levi, Aunt

Blake, and my cousin Moira, Uncle Lenox, Aunt Lily, cousins Carter and Ethan, and this is my Uncle Jasper, Aunt Emily, and their tribe, Jason, Delaney, Quinn, Hadley, and Adalynn."

"Quite a family you have son." The Director looked at Nick's family and smiled. "Lenox, Jasper, Levi, Clark, always a pleasure to see you. I was sorry to hear you all retired. The good guys lost four of our best men. I was happy to hear you'd agreed to continue to train the young bucks. The FBI is looking forward to sending you agents. They will greatly benefit from your expertise."

"Pleasure to see you as well, Tony. We're looking forward to it," Lenox said.

"I'll let you get back to enjoying your family. Nick, I'd like to see you Monday morning. Your first assignment awaits."

"Yes, sir," Nicholas answered, anxious to get to work.

NICK WAS TRYING NOT to choke up as he said goodbye to his family, grateful they'd all made the trip to watch him graduate. He missed them all, even the youngest of his cousins, the twins, Hadley and

Adalynn. Rea had filled him in on the havoc the six-year-olds wreaked around the Walker household. Controlled chaos was what Emily called it.

"Thank you all for coming. Mind if I talk to Nolan alone for a minute?" Nick asked the crowd as they were loading up their cars for the drive back to Georgia.

"Thank you." Nick wasted no time. The longer it took to get the words out, the more of a chance there was he'd tear up.

"No need."

"There is. I want you to know that I know everything you protected me from, everything you gave me. When I was eleven, I was scared and broken, but I still remember all the things you did for me. I know how lucky I am. You're not my uncle; you are so much more. My dad, my mentor, my tutor, my consoler, my friend. I have more than most. You gave me all of them." Nick stopped and pointed toward his family. "You all made me who I am. I want you to know I'll make you proud. And one day I hope to be half the man you are."

"You could never be half the man I am." Clark cleared his throat before he finished. "You're already a better man than I could ever be. And son, you don't need to try and make me proud. I already am.

And not because you worked your ass off and graduated high school with honors, graduated college, and not because you've earned a shield and get to call yourself Special Agent. I'm proud because you are the most resilient and kindest person I know. You were as a boy, and you are as a man. I'm proud you know the value of family. Nicholas, those people over there, your uncles, we have your back. We are your home. In your line of work, as in mine, there will be times when the weight bears down, and you're bending to a breaking point. That is when you need to come home and let us carry the load. We've all had to do it, and there's no shame. I love you." Nick nodded, afraid of his own voice. "Be safe."

"I will."

Nicholas felt every word his uncle had said when they stood in the parking lot of the hotel saying their goodbyes. He knew he meant them too. He'd always have his family waiting to catch him if he needed. That knowledge allowed him to excel in the FBI. He had the freedom to take chances, save lives, and solve cases.

Clark was correct when he told Nicholas there would be a time he'd need to find solace in his family. When that day came, and Nick was on the brink of making the biggest mistake of his life, his uncles stood by his side and held him up.

But that day was four years in the making, and was spent chasing a serial killer; a deranged murderer that had fixated on the woman that held his heart.

THE 707 FREEDOM SERIES IS COMPLETE

Carter Lenox, Jasper Walker, Levi McCoy, and Nolan Clark had finally found the freedom they'd all needed to move on from their pasts, found the women they loved, and as any good man would – they held on. They'd all served their country well, and it was time for them to sit back and enjoy their retirement from the Army. They were starting a new chapter of their lives - reaping the beauty they had created.

THE NEXT GENERATION –

Nicholas Clark, Jason Walker, Carter Lenox, Ethan Lenox, Moira McCoy, Delaney Walker, Jackson Clark, Quinn Walker, Hadley Walker, and Adalynn Walker are all grown up. The next generation is their stories – we step years into the future as each member of the 707 offspring make their tentative steps into adulthood and beyond.

Starting May 2018 with Nick Clark's story – Saving Meadow - mybook.to/savingmeadow

Don't miss the release of Nick's book! Sign up for release notification.
https://www.subscribepage.com/RRsignup

SAVING MEADOW- FIRST LOOK

"Nicholas, just in time." Nick Clark turned, finding himself face-to-face with the man he'd come to see.

"Director," Nick greeted.

"How does it feel walking back in here with a shield and creds?" the director asked, offering Nick his hand.

"Different." Nick took his hand in a firm shake and contemplated his answer.

He did feel different. Not even two days ago he'd walked through these very doors with his family. That had felt different as well, sitting in the front of the graduation hall taking his final oath, alongside the men and women who'd become his comrades. They'd spent the last six months together, training both physically and mentally toward a common goal – the honor to call themselves *Special Agents*.

He'd vowed his service and allegiance, to protect and serve, to honor the office of the FBI. Nick had sworn fidelity, bravery, and integrity. Words he would never forget, the very words that were proudly carved above the entrance to FBI headquarters and every field office across the U.S.

Now, as he stood in front of the building shaking the director's hand, Nick felt the heaviness of his position weighing on him. All his life, Nick knew he wanted to serve, like his uncles. Only the military hadn't appealed to him. He'd watched the toll it took on his uncles: Clark, Lenox, Levi, and Jasper. Every mission they'd completed seemed to take another bite out of their souls. While the men that had raised him and been his mentors were strong enough for that type of service, Nick knew he wasn't. He wanted to help catch the bad guys, lock them up and keep the public safe on the homefront, not fight a war that was unwinnable – not in the immediate. Nick was far too impatient; he liked closure and control. He admired his uncles and knew their service was necessary and selfless, but he'd chosen a different path.

The FBI had been Nick's dream. He found

every part of the criminal mind fascinating, and the process in which the offender was apprehended even more so. The investigation and progression of a case had sparked something deep in Nick at a very young age. He'd been lucky growing up with four men who had taught him to hone his instincts. They'd schooled him on battlefield tactics and weapons safety the moment he'd expressed an interest in law enforcement. His uncles had also walked him through the process of critical thinking and crime scene investigation. While his uncles may have been gathering intel on terrorists in a foreign country, the process was the same.

"Come on. We're meeting with Unit Chief Kilby. He should already be inside."

The director held open the door for Nick to precede him. Once both men were in the building, Nick fell in step beside the director. Instead of going to the second floor where Nick knew the other man's office was located, they continued further into the lobby before turning right and stopping in front of a set of double doors, frosted for privacy and *Behavioral Analysist Unit* etched in the glass.

Nick's brow knitted, and he wondered why the director was taking him to the BAU. Not that he would question the man; Nick wasn't dumb. The director scanned his badge and the lock clicked, allowing the men entrance into what he'd considered the Holy Grail of the FBI, a place that he'd fantasized about being a part of, but knew it would take a master's degree and a decade of hard work to prove his worth before he'd even be considered. The badge clipped to his belt was still shiny and brand new. He couldn't even call it a shield yet, he'd only earned it two days ago. It was silly, but to Nick, it would be a badge until it had some scratches on it, until he could prove himself as a SA.

The room was exactly as he'd known it would be. Not the desks, or office furniture, or the file cabinets that lined the wall, or even the conference room he could see off to the side. It was the energy of the room; it was electric and alive. These men and women dug into the psyche and picked it apart, analyzing a criminal's behavior to reconstruct the unsub's motives, method, and the rationale behind the crime. In other words, Nick thought the profilers with the BAU were brilliant and maybe a little twisted themselves. After all, there had to be a price to pay climbing into the mind of a killer.

"SSA Kilby." the director greeted when they'd approached a tall man in his late forties. "This is SA Clark."

"Yes. Nice to meet you. Let's go into the conference room and talk."

"A pleasure." With a nod, Nick silently followed both men, scanning the office as he went.

When the men were seated around the table, SSA Kilby started. "The director tells me you were the top of your graduating class."

"That is correct, sir."

"Please call me Kilby, everyone else does. We're not big on formalities around here. The director gave me your file. I'm impressed."

"Thank you."

"You scored exceptionally well all around; however, it is the way you processed the mock crime scenes that truly interests me. In all the scenarios you found things your peers had missed. And you analyzed the evidence presented differently as well."

Kilby's praise struck Nick straight in the gut. He didn't often need validation from others but coming from SSA Kilby it meant something to him. However, Nick was mildly uncomfortable, and not knowing what to say, he remained quiet.

Kilby slid an image across the table to Nick. "What is the first thing that comes to mind when you look at that image?"

Nick looked down at the photograph of a grizzly

crime scene; a male and female lying on the floor of a living room, blood pooling around their bodies, staining the carpet. Each had multiple stab wounds. At first glance, he'd say each had to have at least a dozen or more. He continued to scrutinize the image, looking for anything that stood out, nothing did. A family home, modest in the furnishings he could see. Nothing ransacked or displaced, both bodies still clothed, not posed.

"Why?" Nick asked.

"Why?" Kilby's brow pulled up, and he studied Nick from across the table. "Interesting. Explain your question."

"When I look at the crime scene the first thing I want to know is why. Why them? Why that house? Why did the offender use a knife? Why the overkill? What drove the unsub? Once I start there, I can work backwards through the solution matrix. It is easier to build on what I don't know then find the who, what, where, and when. The *why* is what tells the real story."

Kilby and the director exchanged a look before Kilby retrieved a file from the storage credenza behind him. For the first time since Nick entered the room, he took the time to take in his surroundings. A modern black laminate table with brushed aluminum sides, eight high-back leather executive chairs, a matching black storage cabinet, a bank of monitors hung on one wall, a large gold FBI - BAU crest embellished the adjoining wall. Classy, clean, and efficient. Nick sat back in his chair willing himself still, uncertain of what was happening. Oddly he felt like he was in a job interview. Not knowing if he'd passed the impromptu exam or got the job – not that he understood what the job was - was driving him crazy, but he refused to fidget in front of the men.

"Do you know why you're here?" Kilby asked.

"No."

"There is an opening on my team, SA Winters is leaving. He's been asked to teach a class on the taxonomy of human behavior. The director and I have spoken at length about bringing you on the team as his replacement. A fresh set of eyes, no bad law enforcement habits to break, no preconceived bias. We can mold you into what we need. I still have my reservations. However, there is no denying you have a natural instinct that cannot be ignored. I'd like you to look at an ongoing investigation and present a profile and full report."

Before Nick could answer, a manila folder was slid across the table. Nick stopped the dossier with his hand, looking down at it. Once again, his chest filled with pride - Federal Bureau of Investigations: Case File 033077RE neatly stamped on the front. He opened the folder, and his heart rate spiked, and not from the excitement of perusing his first official case. He thought about closing the file and taking a minute to mentally prepare for the image that had assaulted him. He stared at the crime scene photo - a woman lay dead in an alley. Dark hair, age unknown due to multiple stab wounds to her face, height, and weight indeterminable. Nick flipped the image, and the next photograph was worse. A blonde woman, again in an alley; this woman's face was peeling and blistered, her features and age uncertain. Nick flipped through more pages, all women, all with facial disfiguration; blondes, brunettes, red heads, and black hair. All white, all dumped in the open.

When he got to the last image, he turned it over and looked at the men, carefully studying him.

"Eleven women over twelve months," Kilby started. "You'll find the rest of the information at the desk I had cleared for you. I'll introduce you to the team and let you get to work."

What the fuck had just happened? Nick gawked at the unit chief and hoped his mouth wasn't actually hanging open in his stupor.

"Thank you for the opportunity," Nick stammered. "When would you like the profile?"

"Tomorrow. You'll present it to the team at 9 a.m."

Tomorrow? Was Kilby insane? He'd need more than twenty-four hours to properly comb the case and research the terminology and theories he still didn't grasp. He still had so much to learn, ten years' worth of knowledge to be exact, that was the average time it took before an agent was considered.

"Don't over think this. I don't want a textbook profile. I have four highly qualified profilers that have already worked up a report. I want your gut feeling. Tell me the why. Think outside the box."

"I don't know what the box is in this case."

"The box is the textbook profile, look past it. Tell me what we don't know. That's how we'll find this son of a bitch. Stop thinking like Special Agent Nick Clark and get in killer's head; feel it, experience it, what's the fantasy. Then you'll have your composite of the offender."

Wordlessly, Nick stood when the other two men did and followed them back into the central office. Three men and a woman were standing near an empty desk, their conversation coming to a halt as the three men approached.

"Nick Clark this is, Mike Gonzales, Joel Brinkley, Ben Dailey, and Mandy Brown. Your new team."

And that was the beginning of Nick's trial by fire and unconventional introduction to the BAU.

Continue reading - mybook.to/savingmeadow

ACKNOWLEDGMENTS

A special thanks to my Alpha readers – Michelle Thomas and Chriss Prokic, Thank you so much for all your help on this book.

Cindy Wolken – you worked tirelessly on this book. Thank you so very much!

To the BETA readers, reviewers, and Bloggers that took time out of their lives to read, review and promote this project – THANK YOU! As with anything else in life it takes a village. I couldn't have published this book without your help.

Ellie Masters – Thank you. Your friendship, guidance, and steadfast support means the world to me. I wouldn't have finished this book when I did if it wasn't for your word sprints. You truly are one-of-a-kind.

Kendall Barnett – My business partner and friend -You are the bomb dot com. I love you woman!

Chris Genovese and Faith Gibson – The two of you listen to me whine and complain daily about the progress of writing and publishing. You help me when I get stuck and always take time out of your busy schedules to bounce ideas around. But it is your unwavering encouragement that I appreciate the most. It means the world to me to call the two of you my friends.

RILEY EDWARDS NEWSLETTER

Claim your free copy of Unbroken here: https://www.subscribepage.com/rileyedwardsfreebook

Unbroken - A second chance at love story

Five years after my husband's brutal murder, I am still trying to piece my life back together. A series of disastrous events sends, not only my life but my son's life into peril. With everything spiraling out of control, and our safety on the line, I have no choice but to ask my longtime friend, Reid for help. I realize my mistake too late. Reid is all in, and is taking over my life completely. He looks at me like a woman, not a widow or a mother. He makes we wish for things I know I shouldn't have. Just when he opens my eyes to the world around me, and I see the man that has been standing right in front of me all these years - it's too late. One kiss is all I am allowed before my life takes another painful twist and all thoughts of happiness are torn from my reach.

Trust – Season Two

ABOUT THE AUTHOR

Riley Edwards is a bestselling multi-genre author, wife, and military mom. Riley was born and raised in Los Angeles but now resides on the east coast with her fantastic husband and children.

Riley writes heart-stopping romance with sexy alpha heroes and even stronger heroines. Riley's favorite genres to write are romantic suspense and military romance.

Don't forget to sign up for Riley's newsletter and never miss another release, sale, or exclusive bonus material. https://www.subscribepage.com/RRsignup

Facebook Fan Group

www.rileyedwardsromance.com

Made in United States
North Haven, CT
13 January 2024

47422615R00174